# SEMPRE'S RETURN

## BOOK THREE OF 'THE SMITH CHRONICLES'

**JOHN K. IRVINE**

# CONTENTS

Acknowledgements

Dedication

Quotation

Map of Muhaze City


PART ONE
**REAWAKENING**
1



PART TWO
**REVENGE**
105


About The Author
182

# Acknowledgements

To Giacinto Scelsi: Whose music has accompanied the writing of this book. Thank you, maestro, wherever you may be.

To Sam Hayles: For the best cover yet. Thank you, Sam.

To Louise Ironside: For everything. Thank you, Louise.

# Dedication

*For Louise*

# Quotation

*The restful loneliness of the only life he had known was gone. Here the very air was palpitant with life. It hummed and buzzed unceasingly. Continually changing its intensity, and abruptly variant in pitch, it impinged on his nerves and senses, made him nervous and restless, and worried him with a perpetual imminence of happening.*

Jack London - 'White Fang' (1905)

# MUHAZE CITY CENTRE

to Lojikaal Parc

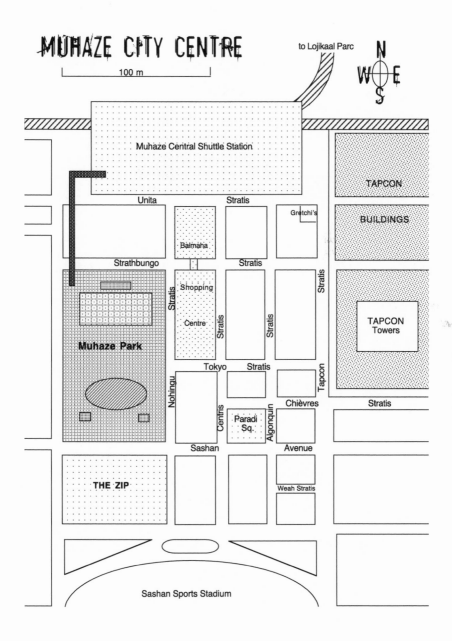

# PART ONE

## 'Reawakening'

## Prologue
*08:35 – 13 October, 2187 (Muhaze, Tapi-36)*

David Sempre roared with anger. A piercing cry of self-loathing and hatred for those that had betrayed him. The scream echoed through the collapsing building and brought down more debris from the ceiling above.

Sempre's mind was in such agony that he felt as if it were closing in on itself; as if his brain was imploding with the weight of this new horror. A horror that made the duality between mind and body all too real, all too extreme.

His head was his, but his body was his mother's.

And though it was the torso of a 60-year-old woman, it was muscular and strong. As if it had been pumped up; inflated. His skin stretched with the ripple of muscle tissue.

He flexed his left arm, then the right - each bicep bulged with a formidable beefiness. The amount of chemicals used to do this must have been enormous.

His limbs had ripped holes through the sleeves of the floral print dress that Mayette Froome had been so fond of wearing; and had still been dressed in, all those years ago when she had been cryogenically frozen.

But why was he like this?

1

Was it someone's idea of a sick joke?

Another detonation went off outside.

Looking around, Sempre quickly realised that he wasn't at TAPCON Towers. He was in the Specialist's bunker out near the Airfield.

But how?

How did he get there?

He tried to piece together his last waking moments, but nothing came.

More muffled explosions went off again, somewhere above him, prompting Sempre to look up at the ceiling. Dust continued to sputter down into the bunker. Some specks floated into his eyes and he blinked to clear his gaze. It was then that he saw the swarm of NITs buzzing in a grotesque huddle of evil, over by the Specialists' workbench. Sempre took a wary step backwards.

The NITs began to flock towards him, slowly at first, then eagerly as if they were strangely attracted to him. Sensing danger, Sempre raised his arms in defence, but it was no use, and soon several hundred of the tiny metal beasts were upon him, buzzing around his head in a fervour. He frantically tried to swat them away, but his efforts were futile.

But yet, they weren't attacking him.

In fact, just the opposite.

They were gathering around him as if they wanted to follow him; as if they wanted to go wherever he went. Like they had chosen him as their leader. Their noise was not aggressive or volatile, rather a compliant hum that if translated into words would say: 'We are at your command - Oh, Great Master'.

Somehow, Sempre sensed this.

He moved a step to his right.

The NITs followed.

He moved back to his left.

The NITs were right there with him.

He swung his arms in circles at his side. The NITs followed his every move; creating a spherical murmuration of nasty mechanical gnats.

Sempre smiled, then said: "NITs... Sempre says: 'Go to the Specialists'."

Immediately the deadly probes flew across the room to

the two bodies on the floor, then waited for their next command.

Sempre's grin widened.

Something moved in the rubble to Sempre's left. One of the Specialist's lab rats had survived the blast. The way it scuttled amongst the detritus instantly reminded Sempre of his old assistant, Flugg. But thinking about Flugg only made him annoyed.

"Sempre says: 'Kill the rat'!" he yelped, his mother's windpipe making him sound like the 'Wicked Witch of the Earth-based West'.

The NITs swarmed down onto the pathetic creature and, in an instant, its brain was punctured by hundreds of proboscises. It was dead.

"Ha!" exclaimed Sempre. Then remembered that he usually laughed in threes: "Ha, ha, ha!" he corrected.

The NITs returned to their master, and hovered expectantly, waiting for further instructions.

Sempre grinned, again. Wider this time. "Oh, this is genius!" he exclaimed. "What power!"

An overwhelming feeling of omnipotence surged through his veins, and again he roared - this time in pure pleasure. But, on hearing his high-pitched scream, he was reminded again of his transformed body.

The thought disgusted him.

He wanted to tear it off and throw it away into a dark corner.

But then Sempre had a thought. Could his *real* body be somewhere around the lab? If this was where the Specialists had brought him after the fall of TAPCON, then maybe the rest of him was here too, somewhere in amongst all the mess and tangled wires.

He began to search the lab for the capsule.

There was so much rubble in the lab that, on first glance, it made Sempre think his task would be somewhat difficult. However, his new strength allowed him to work quickly. Objects that would have previously been impossible for him to lift were now easily picked up and put aside.

After ten minutes of this, Sempre had found nothing. He had almost given up hope. He let out a long frustrated sigh that filled the room.

But in the silence that followed, he heard a low beeping noise. It was coming from the far corner of the lab. It got louder as he approached and there, underneath a large sheet of metal, he saw a glint of Actionglass.

He quickly removed the metal and swept away the dust from the surface of the glass. He knew instantly that this was it. It was still plugged in - he could see the white gas from the cooling system circulating inside the pod.

Sempre pushed the remaining bits of junk off of the capsule and found the button at the side that opened the lid. He pressed it, and the lid slid back. The white vapour came out with such force that he was almost knocked over. But then, as it dissipated, he could see his headless body lying there on the plinth, still in his old grey suit. His mother's head was at his side. Both were connected with wires and sensors, and were obviously still in cryro-animation. The pod beeped a warning and a red light came on. Sempre closed the lid quickly, the side catches fastening automatically as he did so. The light continued to flash and a computer voice was calmly repeating: "Unathourised opening, please wait for security." He turned towards the Specialists' bodies, a snarl coming to his lips.

*They must have brought me here. Mitchell and Quince. From the rubble of the Towers. But how was I put in the pod?*

A hazy memory came to him…

*Tamashito was looking at me from outside of Mother's casket. I remember he looked just like Herra, with his beard. Yes! He must have done it! He must have knocked me out and put me in the pod. Who else was there? And I was cold. So very cold. Then… nothing. A blank. Until now. But what have I become? Why have they done this to me?*

He felt a horrific anger surge through his body. It was so strong he felt like his veins would burst; as if his body would simply explode with the pressure.

He roared again, and this time even the NITs seemed to cower at the sheer primacy of his scream. Sempre no longer cared what it sounded like. All he could think of was his revenge.

The Specialists had already paid with their lives, and

4

now it was time that he let Dr. Tamashito, and the rest of the universe, know how he felt about them.

# Chapter 1

Ignacio Phinn was on the box:

*'The 'Golden Circuit', as it's called, is all around us. Some scientists say that it's a physical impossibility, that it's a hoax. But that hasn't stopped hundreds of people taking to social-space media with clips of themselves moving objects and blasting rocks. It seems that everyone has one in their family now. Unknowingly, Mikita Smith seems to have started the craze of the millennium - but she is mysteriously nowhere to be found. Since her much publicised run-in with The Oort Cloud Cult she's simply vanished. And now her thousands of fans are wondering if she's actually dead. Further to this report, we have learned that the IFS has today pledged new support for these individuals. The report is coming up next with Harriet Honeste...'*

Kané Smith shook his head and pressed the mute button on the remote, then threw the control onto the nearby sofa. He looked at the tab of Nanoloxetin on Polo's living room table. He looked at it, <u>lovingly</u>.

*Just the one,* he told himself. *That's all I need, then I'll stop again.*

A junkie's reasoning. Deep down, Kané knew it was a lie; he knew it wasn't going to be like that. He'd have the tab, enjoy the hit and then come down from his high. Then he'd need another one, and another, and soon he'd be back in Grafuulen, knocking on darkened doors asking for more pills and running up another massive loan with some shark. But this rational thinking was pushed to the back of his mind, like a twinkling star at the other end of the galaxy, as Kané told himself to take the tab and consider the consequences later.

He picked up the pill...

"What the mighty shizz are you playing at, Kané!?"

Polo came into the front room (new suit, hat and tie) and was stopped dead in her tracks by what she saw.

Kané got up guiltily, and knocked the table over. His stuff flew in every direction: "No, wait, Polo, it's not what you think, I was just going to -"

But Polo was already over to him and grabbing the Nanoloxetin from the floor before he could finish his sentence.

"Holy draining Herra, Kané, I thought we'd agreed that you were going to stay clean?" She immediately got out her meta-file. "I'm phoning Dr. Rexian right now."

Polo punched some numbers into her device, all the while watching Kané like an Earth-based hawk. He was still protesting his innocence when Dr. Rexian, the Smith family doctor, came on the line.

"Hello, Dr. Rex? It's Polo Smith here.... Yes, we're all well, thanks... No, she's not dead... On holiday, yeah, that's right. Listen, Doc, my brother Kané needs some help. Can you see him today?"

Kané shook his head. It seemed like Polo had become his mother recently - though she looked more like his father, in those suits she wore all the time.

"Twelve o'clock? That's great. Thanks, Doc. He'll see you then."

Kané was still shaking his head, but now it was at his own stupidity. "Why did I open my door to you in Grafuulen?"

Polo gave him a look. "You opened it because you secretly wanted my help, that's why."

"C'mon, Po. Just let me have that tab. It's my last one. I swear I'll stop after that. I'll have to anyways, I've got no money."

"Well, be that as it may, you still need to see the Doc. Then you need to get a job. Then you need to get some order in your life, some consistency. You really need to try harder, Kané. You really need to work at it. You need to get yourself free from the stuff that's holding you back in life."

She held up the tab, then left the room. "I'm putting it somewhere you'll never find it."

After a few seconds Polo came back to the living room.

"There. You're done with them."

Kané knew that Polo was right, but that didn't stop him craving the Ns.

"Look, after we go to the doctor's, we'll go do something nice together. We know he's going give you some Dromadone, to relieve the withdrawal, then after that we'll go see a film. That new Nigel-666 thing. It might take your mind off all of this."

Kané nodded. "Yeah, sure, Polo. Sounds good. Whatever you want."

Polo paused, and looked at her cousin. He was a mess. "Look. It's just you and me now, Kané. Mikita's gone. Gone for good, I reckon. She'll get married to Zanthu and that'll be it. Alien babies, more travelling around the universe -"

"Yeah, you're right, Po."

Polo glanced wistfully at her new Comms device - the one Mikita had given her before she left; the one made by Marcie on Plaateux-5. She tried to will it to turn on - to light up with a message from Mikita telling her she was on her way back to Tapi-36. That she'd missed Polo so much, she'd decided to call it off with Zanthu and come home.

Kané saw her looking at the machine. "You miss her, huh?"

Polo nodded, then went over to the shelf, took down the small Comms device and placed it in her suit pocket.

"I'm sure she misses you too, Po. You were… *are* her best friend, you know."

Polo smiled at Kané. She was so struck with this rare show of kindness. Then she saw Kané's eyes dart to the hallway and back again to meet her gaze.

"Oh no, I'm not falling for that," she said, backing up and standing spread-eagled between him and the doorway.

"Oh, come on, Po. Just let me have it? Please?"

"No way, Kané!" Polo turned quickly and headed for her bedroom.

Kané fumed. He had a good mind to follow her.

He looked at the TV. Harriet Honeste was interviewing a woman with a weird baby, that stared, wide-eyed at the camera - the caption underneath read 'Baby controls family dog with golden powers.'

Kané grinned. "Hey, Polo? Don't make me use the GC on you now."

Polo stuck her head back around the door. "You what? The GC? Don't make me laugh. You've not used that since you burnt down the - sorry, since 'the incident'."

What could Kané say? Polo was right. He'd not used the Golden Circuit since he was a boy. He hated it. The things it did. The trouble it made. Not to mention the pain it caused him when he <u>did</u> use it. "Well, I could if I really wanted to."

Polo shook her head. "Yeah, right." She disappeared again, down the hall as she continued her put-down: "You'd be about as much good as the bozos you're watching on TV."

Kané rolled his eyes, then sat back down on the couch. He felt a twinge of nausea in his stomach - the pangs of withdrawal were beginning. His mind flickered to a rare, dark thought:

He could use physical force to get the drugs off Polo.

He closed his eyes and shook away the notion. What kind of animal would do such a thing - harm someone just to get to his drugs? What would that make him? For all his self-hatred, he couldn't let himself sink that low. Polo was his cousin, for Herra's sake. He lay back on the sofa, closed his eyes, and waited for the withdrawal to carry out its vengeful ways.

## Chapter 2

The Peers were waiting in the Argon's Holding quarters. Their parents were due to arrive in a few hours, the IFS having sent them a spacecraft, the Turandot, to dock with the Argon for a photo opportunity, and then an announcement that they were to become Special Ambassadors for the IFS. Their job would be to spread awareness of their gifts, and make sure that people understood they weren't freaks; that they were normal people who just so happened to have been given an ability - like being good at sports, drawing or math.

The IFS had sent a document to all solar bodies under their jurisdiction to observe and respect the abilities of GC wielders everywhere, and to protect them from the ills and prejudices of their respective societies. The IFS also stated that they were now investigating the scientific origins of the Golden Circuit. They wanted to 'uncover the processes and forge new links with wielders across the universe for the benefit of all mankind'. A new Institute was being setup on Mars that would spearhead research into the phenomenon.

*

Captain Phil Jameson's interest in the Peers was genuine

10

- his daughter was one of them. But nobody was sure where she was, though there was a rumour she had gone with the Code, Zanthu, and was on their starship the Krashaon. Jameson knew the truth, of course, but he wasn't going to let the media ruin his daughter's happiness. He put down the IFS document and put his feet up on the Stateroom table. Eugene Samms, Commander in Chief of the IFS, was on his screen.

"I presume that these rumours are true, Jameson? Your daughter is with the Codes, on their vessel?"

"I have no idea, Commander. After the episode with the Guardians our main concern was with the rehabilitation of Holly Dreamo."

"But you were with her last, when the Peers came aboard your ship?"

"Yes, sir."

"And you did not say 'goodbye' to your own flesh and blood?"

Jameson paused. "Why are you so interested in Mikita, sir?"

"Well, in case you've had your head in the sand, Jameson, she is quite a story. Since we released the data to the press concerning the Golden Circuit, her appeal has become considerable. And, added to this, is the mystery of her disappearance."

"You haven't answered my question, sir."

Samms exhaled. "Enough of this. I want to talk to you about more important things - the Tapi-36 power plant. I need you behind this 100%, Jameson. Do I have that? Can I rely on you to see this through to the end without any problems?"

The Captain's eyes flashed. "Commander, Tapi-36 should not be seen as an Earth-based guinea pig for the whims of the IFS. No matter how honourable."

A look of innocence broke out across Samms' grey, weathered face. "No, no, Jameson. You are entirely correct. But we don't see the plans as being a 'whim'. On the contrary. Now that Janeee Swish has become President it is an ideal opportunity to start afresh. I can assure you, the power station is completely safe. Trials were run on Mars for the past 15 years and there has never been an incident in all that time."

"Never been a *major* incident, is what you mean, sir."

"No need to split hairs, Jameson."

"Not when you can split atoms, Commander."

Samms smiled at the witticism. "You are a very clever fellow, Jameson. And that's why we want you to oversee this project. We know that you were not best pleased with TAPCON and its methods - and in hindsight we at the IFS see it as an error of judgement. David Sempre was a mistake. An aberration. We underestimated his levels of insanity. They were profound. A complete psychopath. But, there it is…"

Jameson thought that it was unusual for Samms to be so introspective.

The CINC continued: "But sometimes I wonder about you, Phil. I wonder whether you are truly… with us?"

Jameson answered quickly. "Commander, I have worked all my life for the IFS and the space program. It is all I have, and all I wish to have. I do harbour reservations about a power station positioned so close to a major city, this is true. And I would like to know the power source in full detail. There has been nothing about this in the brief. But, done correctly, I can't see any real objections, in theory -"

"Good, I'm glad to hear it," interrupted Samms. "But I must be sure of your loyalty, you understand. And that's why, Jameson, I'm sending Reg Spalding to assist you."

Jameson's face blanched.

"I want you to work with him - get this station up and running, as quickly as possible. I believe he's on his way to you now. You'll meet him at the Lumiol-S3 Apex. He'll fill you in on the details. The Starship Turandot will be following on behind Spalding's craft, with the GC wielders' relatives onboard, then the handover of the youngsters will take place. A photo opportunity, in essence. You understand these things, Captain."

"Yes, sir."

"Well, Good luck, Jameson. I'm counting on you."

The screen went to snow.

Jameson turned away.

*Reg Shizzing Spalding,* he thought. *That's all I draining need.*

"Something wrong, Captain?" said a female voice, at

the door.

It was McGilvary, his second-in-command.

Jameson looked up. "No, no. Nothing, Lieutenant. Nothing at all."

He got out of his seat and forced a rather formal look.

"McGilvary gather the crew. Team huddle in 30 minutes on the bridge. I want everyone there, got me?"

"Yes, sir," said McGilvary, and left quickly. She knew when the Captain meant business - it was when he started using Earth-based sports metaphors.

Alone again in the Stateroom, Jameson shook his head. *Reg Shizzing Spalding...* he repeated.

A bureaucrat's bureaucrat.

An administrator's administrator.

A middleman's middleman.

In other words, the lowest form of life.

Jameson had butted heads with Spalding on a several occasions during his career and each time Jameson had come out on the losing end - the Moonsmen group, the troubles on Yolanda CDI - every single time Spalding wiped the floor with him.

Spalding was an inherently vain man, whose narcissism drove him to achieve profound levels of success. Known throughout the cosmos as a royal pain-in-the-Earth-based-derrière, Spalding would sell his grandmother for a wooden nickel if he thought it would seal the deal. And no metaphorical dog would remain un-kicked in the course of his single-minded pursuit of sorting out the hounds from the pedigrees. His co-workers lived in fear of his bullying tactics, and it was his sheer arrogance and sense of entitlement that made others crumble beneath him and give in to his demands. That, and the fact that he had a 24/7 direct-line to Eugene Samms.

Jameson wasn't good with accepting those kind of feelings. They made him edgy.

And now, he needed coffee.

With milk.

And two sugars.

And a cookie, with chocolate on top.

## Chapter 3
*10:02 - 13 October, 2187 (Muhaze, Tapi-36)*

David Sempre was readjusting himself to his new physical form. It seemed to be in a state of flux, and this in turn affected his emotions. Anger appeared suddenly and took over his senses, leaving him unable to control it. The episode would last for a while, then subside, leaving him dazed and anxious. Then, his strength would disappear, leaving him weak and flaccid. This would soon pass and he would find himself again with the strength of a hundred Earth-based lions. It left him confused and disturbingly unpredictable, but he was a man (or a woman, depending on how you looked at it) with a mission, and despite his mental condition, Sempre was determined to get his revenge on those that had wronged him.

Sempre knew his way around the bunker. He'd been there before, once or twice. The lab was connected to the outside world by a tunnel that led in one direction up to the Airfield itself, and in the other, to the main buildings further along the passage. As he made his way down the corridor to the surface hatch, doors would simply break off when he pushed them. As much as he enjoyed this newfound strength, it worried him too.

Soon he was at the duct leading upward to the entrance used most frequently by The Specialists. They never liked to go through the Airfield buildings. Not if the didn't have to. Associating with the *hoi polloi* was not their idea of a good time, and they always kept that entrance locked and fully encrypted to ensure they were the only ones who could gain access. Luckily for them, no one from the Airforce wanted to go into the bunker anyway. The Specialists were just too draining weird, too shizzing strange for the likes of Airforce personnel.

Sempre climbed the metal ladder to the top of the surface shaft. Once there, he simply forced the round hatch up and out. Breaking it off in the process.

Light streamed into the tunnel and blinded him for a moment.

As he stepped out onto the airfield, dust was all around him, enveloping his body, and covering his already mucky face in grot. The NITs hovered below him in the conduit, waiting impatiently to be given an order. The sound of machinery rang in his ears, and through the clouds of dust he saw diggers moving soil, and cranes swinging wrecking balls. He took a step towards the noise and noticed that men in hard hats were shouting orders, and trucks were moving in and out through the dusty air carrying huge chunks of building.

They were knocking down the airfield.

His airfield!

What he didn't know was that the IFS were planning to replace it with a highly controversial power plant. He also didn't know that the IFS saw him as an embarrassment and that they were now getting rid of every last visual remnant of his reign as President.

What Sempre was also in ignorance of was the fact that the IFS thought he was dead (as did the rest of the populace of Tapi-36) and that he wasn't President anymore.

Now that would have made him really upset.

Sempre was furious that they were dismantling what he had spent so long planning. The Airfield was part of a long line of architectural wonders that he'd wanted to leave behind as his legacy. The whole re-building project was his father's idea, right enough, but it was carried out in his own image. The sight before him was all too much for Sempre.

Nevertheless, a knowing smile soon came across his filthy face.

"NITs?" he said. "Sempre says: 'Kill them all!'"

Upon the order, the NITs dispersed, the awful humming noise increasing in volume as they surged towards the machinery and its operators.

The workman had no time to realise what was happening. It took about 20 seconds for all the NITs to complete their task. The cries of agony were brief, their deaths, immediate.

The machinery had now stopped, and as the dust cleared, Sempre surveyed the scene. His smile turned once again to a concentrated look of anger.

The workmen had completely flattened his airfield.

Who had given these orders?

Who had wanted to destroy this architectural jewel?

Over near the building site offices, two men came out of the temporary builds. Sempre saw them. They were pointing at him. One of them hurried back inside the offices.

"NITs? Sempre says: 'Finish the job!'"

A few of the swarm set off to the outhouses. Sempre watched as the remaining man ran for cover. But soon enough he heard two screams of agony, and knew that the NITs had done their work. They returned quickly to their master's shoulder and Sempre found himself in the eerie silence once again.

He closed his eyes and took a deep breath. He felt the anger subside and noticed that he was thinking clearly; his body once again fluctuating between extremes.

"Now, my little friends," he said to the NITs, "it is time for us to get back what is mine."

Sempre turned and began to walk, slowly (it was as fast as his mother's legs would let him), in the direction of downtown Muhaze.

## Chapter 4
*10:24 - 13 October, 2187 (Starship Krashaon, Michael 6 Quadrant)*

Marcie's device was working perfectly, but Mikita couldn't for the life of her get through to Polo. All she got was a message saying: ERROR... NO SUCH DEVICE EXISTS. She'd only wanted to send Polo a message saying she was fine, that she'd made it safely to the Krashaon, but it looked like it was a no go. She would have to try again later.

Marta, Mikita's young muidog, scampered about on the floor with a tiny rubber ball, oblivious to all her troubles. "It's OK for you, Marta. Just a puppy without a care in the world."

Mikita door buzzed, then opened onto her room.

It was Zanthu. He was speaking with someone in the corridor: "No, I won't, Yastray. It is not possible. Good day." Zanthu entered the room. Mikita went to him.

"What's happening? I'm getting you into trouble, aren't I?"

"Yes. Yes, you are." Zanthu smiled. "But you are worth it."

Mikita sighed. "Maybe I should go home, Zanthu. That would solve a lot of your problems. With me gone."

"No. Listen, Mikita. My people will see reason. They are simply in a state of shock over my father's death. He

17

was their leader for 23 years. It is a long time to be ruled by one person. Times change, and our race needs new blood, new ideas. It is a silly law that prohibits Golden Circuit users access to top office positions. It is based on fear, and fear alone. I will change that, once I am given the power."

"And how does Leylaan feel about you taking his line of honour? He will miss his chance to be Leader."

"Leylaan does not want the responsibility. Nor can he have it. He is like you, Mikita, a wielder. But you know him. You know how he loves his books and his studying. He is not meant for office, even if he was a 'normal' Code. I am different, Mikita. I want to be a leader."

Zanthu moved closer to Mikita and took her in his arms. "Just wait, Mikita. You will see. Things will be fine. I promise."

There was a knock on the door. Zanthu went to answer it. "Mikita, stay here for now. It is probably not a good idea for you to show face at the moment."

Mikita nodded, but inside felt like she was being sidelined.

Zanthu opened the door.

It was Yastray, again.

"Zanthu, my friend. You must come, now, the Heads of State are gathering at the Meeting Place. You must come, but I warn you, be prepared for difficulties. The Senate is not happy. There are many rumblings of discontent -amongst them and amongst the people. This is bad, Zanthu. You have stirred the hornet's nest."

"Yes, Yastray. I understand. I will come immediately."

Yastray didn't move, he was expecting Zanthu to come with him right then and there. Zanthu tilted his head towards the inside of the cabin, intimating Mikita's presence. "Yastray, give me two minutes, my friend."

His comrade fixed him with a look, his face tensed.

Zanthu closed the door. He turned to Mikita. "I must go. There is trouble, but I will make it right. Trust me, Mikita." He made to leave.

"Zanthu?"

"Yes?"

"I love you."

"And I you."

He opened the door, and was gone.

Mikita looked at Marta. The muidog was still wagging her tail and playing with her ball in the corner of the room.

Mikita went back to her Marcie-made Comms device. She tried Polo again, but the screen gave up the same old message: ERROR... NO SUCH DEVICE EXISTS.

Mikita turned off the device and went over to Marta. The muidog leapt up onto Mikita's lap and snuggled in to her stomach.

Mikita began to think she was cursed. Everywhere she went, trouble seemed to rear its ugly head. She looked back on the main points of her existence:

Her childhood: a mess.

Hanoi: a complete mess.

The Guardians: even more of a mess.

And now, Zanthu: another mess - just not happened yet.

Why had she come with Zanthu? Why had she come so far from home not knowing when or if she would ever return? Yes, she loved him, but was that a good enough reason? Her heart and her mind had told her 'yes'. But that didn't necessarily mean it was the right thing to do.

*

The Meeting Place was located on the top deck of the Krashaon. A circular area with a dragonfly image inlaid in the stone floor, shielded with an enormous dome of glass. All around were the planets and stars of the Michael-6 Quadrant; yours to gaze upon as the Krashaon sped on in search of a new home for the Codes. A home where they could begin again. Make a new start and re-learn their linking ways.

But the Codes were traditionalists, despite their experimental nature, and now with Zanthu arriving back with the intention of making Mikita his bride (and thus female Head of State) the issues that had once led to Leylaan leaving his people reared their head once more.

"Council, we are gathered here today, in the shadow of our dear, departed brother, Qaanhu X, to once again address the issue of wielders being allowed to enter into positions of power within our communities."

The speaker was Johaar Zeldine, head Elder of the Codes. His bushy, grey eyebrows sat upon his forehead like two Earth-based porcupines battling each other for territorial ground. He was slightly stooped with age and his grey hands had soft, delicate skin of a man who have never done any manual work, except shuffle paper across a desk and turn pages of learned historical books. The translucency of the Codes was even more present in him. His eyes were violet, the whites yellowing. He wore the traditional garb - jerkin and kilt - and his once blonde hair had now turned white. His unique Scyfer lay exposed on a sun-spotted chest that rattled with phlegm as he spoke. His countenance was, to put it mildly, somewhat dismal.

All the Elders were present: Kongh Luu, Crane CCC and Lukas Rembry III. Each one old, severe and decrepit, like Zeldine. Each one represented the conservative, unwavering discipline of Code culture. Not a smile or sense of humour between them. In fact, there was an old joke amongst other races in the Michael 6 quadrant that went:

*'Ah, yes, The Codes! A smile, a song and a massive starship... Well, one out of three's not bad.'*

There was no denying their reputation of being overly formal and set in their ways, but they did have hidden passions. Their animals were once a prime example. But now that TAPCON had robbed them of this, they were even more inclined to close ranks on their traditions and beliefs. It was all they had left. The two animals they did have: the muidogs, Spoolu and Marta, had both been saved by Mikita Smith, the very person they were about to discuss.

Zeldine continued: "It is not a matter that will take us long, I am convinced of that. The answer is simple. The Golden Circuit is not to be tampered with. Using the life force of the Universe, especially for one's own gains, is sinful."

Kongh Luu joined in: "And Zanthu has not yet taken part in his Reckoning. He has not even attended his first year at the Acoustika Institute. What kind of leader would he be, I ask you!"

Then Crane CCC: "His intended bride is an Earthling

ancestor. The most hopeless race in the entire Solar System!"

Zanthu's face crimsoned with anger, and his violet eyes darkened to a deep purple.

Lukas Rembry III put in the final blow: "I must remind you, Zanthu, that your brother Leylaan, was sent from us. Cast out. It is well known that your mother, Gertrudia, was carrier of this misbegotten gene. Her family line is responsible. Leylaan is back here now, we were wrong to send him away, to those... those... Guardians." A look of shame came over Rembry III's face. "But he is still a wielder. And now both your positions for succession are very badly placed."

A hubbub from the crowd, told Zeldine that the people seemed to agree with what had been said. He continued: "Let us refer to our sage, Dromo. Let him speak to us in the voices of our ancestors. He will tell us the beliefs from olden times." Zeldine signaled to an old man sitting at the corner of the platform "Come Dromo. Come and let us hear the wisdom of the ancients."

Dromo appeared through the crowd. He was a short little man of about 70 years. He was very thin and his clothes hung off him like someone who had lost weight and had not been bothered to buy new garments. He walked as if in a continual trance, his eyes fixed on some distant object. The crowd of Codes parted as he walked towards the roster. He bowed to the Elders and turned to face the audience.

"Now, Dromo," began Johaar. "Please, tell us what the Great Ones say. Scribe? Notate, if you please."

A long-haired scribe had his tablet ready.

Dromo extended his arms and after 10 seconds of silence his face began to turn a pinkish colour. His eyes went up into the top of his head. And his mouth opened, lips trembling with the effort it seemed to cause him. Then Dromo began to mutter: "Esqua, tull ishgi holo foriem mau? Esqua, tull ishgi hanno mei lienad reme esiuol? Gravix volt yuring jay nisten revero. Foriem mau! Foriem mau! Foriem mau!"

Dromo collapsed into a heap at the foot of the steps. His body shook as if convulsed in pain. Several Codes from the audience rushed to help the old man.

Johaar looked pleased with the words he had just heard. His face bore a self-satisfied smile.

"Thank you, Dromo. Now we have heard the words. The scribe will translate."

The scribe stood up and addressed the hall, slowly: "Dromo has said the following words of the Great Ones: 'You ask us, should those touched be cast out? You ask us, should those with powers unnatural be allowed to serve? You will incur grave consequences should you do so. Cast out! Cast out! Cast out!'"

The audience applauded and began to chant: "Cast out! Cast out! Cast out!"

Johaar raised his hands to quiet his people. "We need no more convincing, my people. We are all in agreement with the Ancient ones."

He turned to face Zanthu, who had been listening with mounting anger.

"Zanthu, the Ancient ones have spoken. Do you need more proof? It is clear that your union is not thought of favourably with the masters, nor with us."

Zanthu was fighting himself inside, so as not to publicly humiliate himself with a show of petulance.

"Johaar, Elders. I hear the words and understand that they are spoken in faith. But surely, there must be time for change. There must a time when the rules of the past are not sacrosanct. We must move in current times. We must adapt as a people or face the inevitable; the fact that we are an antiquated people, stuck in the past. Look where following blindly has got us. We now seek a new home. Our animals, they are all dead except for the ones saved by Mikita, my future bride. She is the one who has helped us. With her skills. By using the Golden Circuit. Surely, you cannot turn a blind eye to this fact. We have her, and those who wield, to thank for this."

Johaar looked dismissive. "Zanthu. You have spoken well, your father would be proud of you, but you are mistaken on both counts. We are grateful to Mikita Smith for what she did, but it was her people who slaughtered our animals, we cannot ever forgive someone whose tribe has caused so much pain to ours. And, secondly, the old rules are everything to us. They are the core of our society. We are still alive, we have our Krashaon, the people are all well and healthy, this is all we need. Our values have stayed constant, and this is the reason we are still flourishing as a race." Johaar faced the hall. "My people. We will soon find a new home. We will start again. It will take time but what else is there but time? The Elders have decided, have we not gentlemen?"

Johaar turned to the other grey men with him on the platform. They all nodded in agreement.

"Then, it is done. Your marriage will *not* be allowed. And as for your actions on Baal-500, you will be sent to the seminary for one year. During this time of reflection and servitude to the Priests, you will endeavour to see your failings to your race in a clear light. You will leave tomorrow morning."

Zanthu was incredulous. "A year? But, Johaar. Elders. Please, listen! You must reconsider -"

Johaar held up a hand to silence him. "No, Zanthu. We have spoken. The Ancients have spoken. We are all in accordance. Our word is final."

Zeldine bowed to the audience who in turn bowed back. He left the platform with a nod of politeness and finality towards Zanthu. The audience waited until he had gone, then quietly filed out of the Meeting Place.

And so, it was over. Just like that.

Zanthu was left alone in front of the platform.

He remembered his father had told him that the Elders would not treat him with any bias. It seemed to Zanthu that his father's words had been an understatement.

23

## Chapter 5
*10:44 - 13 October, 2187 (Starship Argon, Michael 6 Quadrant)*


Jameson and the Argon crew were going over preparations for the Peers photo opportunity, the discussion was coming to a conclusion, but Jameson had saved the worst 'til last.

"And so, my final bit of news is that Reg Spalding will be assisting us with the power station management procedures. He'll be here in a five hours."

There was a collective moan from the crew.

Jameson frowned. "Now look, I will not tolerate any attitude, people."

"Oh, c'mon, Captain," said Cox. "With all due respect, sir, Reg Spalding is a... a..."

"A complete shizz on a rope?" interrupted Lead-Out.

"Lead-Out!" intoned Jameson. "Please - we will put our past issues with Mr. Spalding behind us and carry out the IFS programme to the best of our abilities. And that is the end of it. Now, let's get this spacecraft into ship-shape, yes? There is a lot of new equipment on board, so I want double checks on everything to ensure it's all working smoothly for when Spalding gets here. You know how he likes to lay it on thick if anything is out of place." Jameson cut things short. "OK, four hours and fifty-nine minutes and counting, people. Let's get to work."

As the crew made their way back to their posts, McGilvary turned to the Captain. "Will Spalding be staying on board with us, sir?"

"That was not made clear to us, McGilvary, his craft is arriving separately from the Turandot. But let's presume the worst. Get Private Sawchuk to prepare a room for him. Not too close to mine, OK?" Jameson grinned.

McGilvary's knowing smile said it all. "Loud and clear, sir," she replied.

\*

As part of her brief, Dr. Tina Gössner was to provide pastoral care for the Peers. She'd only managed a few sessions with them, but already she'd realised what a burden the GC was to them. They felt the strain of being different from other people all too keenly. She felt sorry for the wielders, especially after all they had been through with Aldoorin Anoote and the Guardians. She had asked to see the group one more time before they met with their parents and the press.

"So, Peers. It won't be long now until you're to be reunited with your parents," began Dr. Tina Gössner. "How are you feeling about that... Cy?"

"A bit nervous, doctor."

"Oh, why is that?"

"Well, I've not seen them for so long. And now that we are... celebrities... I don't know, it'll just be weird, I guess."

"I'm looking forward to seeing my parents," said Tora Arottora. "I've really missed them."

Newton Crash grinned. "I'm looking forward to seeing the Turandot. It's supposed to be massive!"

"And indeed it is," replied Tina.

"Dr. Gössner?" (It was Marcie Llanethli).

"Yes, Marcie?"

"Where's Holly? Can we see her?"

"Holly is in security. She is resting. She's been through a lot recently and needs to have time to reassess her

25

situation. And we need time too. To make sure that she has the best care possible. You may be able to see her at some point before we dock with the Turandot, but I wouldn't get your hopes up too high."

Marcie nodded.

"Now, I don't need to tell you that the Argon is a non-GC wielding craft, so please refrain from using your skills in all parts of the spaceship. You have all become Ambassadors for the Golden Circuit, whether you like that or not. It is important now to act accordingly, beyond your years. I know that will be hard, but we will help you come to terms with that. We're here to support you."

"What will happen to us, Dr. Gössner?" asked Tora Arottora.

Tina smiled. "Well, I imagine that the IFS will want you to work with their scientists, to help them understand how the GC operates. It will be very beneficial to the human race, in the long run. And there seems to be more people claiming to have the ability popping up each day."

"Linden says they are hoaxers," said Cy.

"They are," replied Linden Hoon. "Just wanting to get their faces on TV."

"Well, I'm sure that after all the press coverage goes away so will the people who aren't telling the truth."

The Peers nodded at what Tina had said. She had a way of making everything seem calm and unthreatening. All the Peers liked her.

"Where's Mikita, Dr. Gössner?" asked Newton.

"And where's Leylaan?" asked Cy.

"Linden, would you like to tell them what you have heard?" asked Tina.

Linden Hoon pushed his specs back into position and began, quietly. "Well, as far as I know Leylaan is on the Krashaon. And I must say, I do miss him… terribly. But it is what it is." Linden pushed his specs again. "As far as Mikita is concerned, I also believe she is there on the Code ship. I gather she is to marry Zanthu."

The Peers couldn't contain themselves.

"Oh, how exciting!" said Marcie.

"How romantic," said Tora.

"How soppy," said Cy.

Tina laughed, then turned to Linden. "Thank you,

Linden. We appreciate you telling us this news, and we are sorry that Leylaan cannot be here."

"Thank you, Dr. Gössner. So am I."

"And in trusting us with this information, we must in turn keep this information secret. There are many in the press, and out with, who would dearly like to have this knowledge. So I warn you now, if asked, you will reply you know nothing of either Leylaan's or Mikita's whereabouts. Is that understood, Peers?"

"Yes, Dr. Gössner," they all replied.

"You can trust us," said Marcie.

Tina smiled. "I know I can. Thank you, Marcie." Tina got up. "Our rendezvous with the Turandot will be in approximately four and a half hours. You should all get yourselves ready, and don't forget to put on the IFS uniforms. There is to be a big photograph taken with you, Captain Jameson, Mr. Spalding, and the crew, so you need to look your best. OK?"

"Yes, Dr. Gössner," said the Peers.

"Then later today we leave for Tapi-36 where you'll be interviewed for TV. Then... well, after that I would imagine Mr. Spalding has plans for you." Tina paused, wondering what they would be, she hadn't been informed about where the Peers would go next. "Anyway, I'm sure you'll all be wonderful. Good luck, everyone."

The Peers thanked Tina, then got up and left for their quarters. Their excitement was infectious and even Tina was feeling nervous for some reason. Maybe not nervous, but for some reason she felt... apprehensive. Something was needling at her about the whole set up. She suspected it had something to do with Reg Spalding's arrival.

*Reg Spalding,* she said, to herself. *Wherever he goes, trouble soon follows...*

## Chapter 6
*10:58 - 13 October, 2187 (Muhaze, Tapi-36)*

Sempre found himself at the far western edge of the Airfield. The land here was derelict. The Froome bombing had destroyed everything from the Airfield all the way into the centre of the city where the TAPCON Headquarters had stood. Some parts were better than others, and some rebuilding was already underway, but it made Sempre angry that his vision of the city, his architectural vision had been completely obliterated.

As he trudged on, rubble gradually became road, and soon enough those roads became streets. Sempre knew he was back in <u>his</u> city. His old stomping ground. Despite all the demolition, it still felt good to be back home.

*

The city centre was carrying on its business just like any other metropolis in the Michael 6 Quadrant. Its citizens were happy now. Happier than they'd been for years. Muhazians were out shopping, eating, drinking and generally indulging themselves as they liked to do.

Janeee Swish had replaced that funny looking short man whose name it was hard to remember and was doing a very good job, as far as they could tell. The TV was back on air, the shops were well-stocked and Nigel-666 had a new album and a new film out. What could be better? Yes, things were indeed rather great. But if they only knew what was currently coming their way from the eastern part of the city, they would have thought twice about their current situation.

Unfortunately for them, Muhazians hardly ever thought once.

*

David Sempre must have looked very disturbing. They were used to alien life in Muhaze, but this was a weirdly different proposal. A creature, half male, half female, muscles bulging out of a torn flowery dress. Dirty, sweaty, blood seeping out of his stitches at his neck, the NITs hovering about him like he had some strange disease that attracted flies. It was no wonder that passersby turned and stared.

Sempre heard them whispering:

'What is that?'

'Is that a man, or a woman?'

'I recognise him… her… um, is it a person? Or is it a mutant?'

'He's got fleas! Look at them flying around his head!'

His lips curled into a snarl as he walked past these kibitzers. Soon, they were getting out of his way, some not meeting his gaze until they were past, then they turned and had a good old Muhazian stare.

Sempre marched on. His eye fell on a working megatron across the street. On it was a picture of Janeee Swish, her name was written in a caption underneath - alongside that were the words. 'President of Tapi-36'.

Sempre's brow furrowed. He stopped in his tracks.

"What in Herra's name?" he said out loud. "But I'm the President of Tapi-36."

Sempre listened as Janeee was being interviewed by Harriet Honeste: "And because of TAPCON's abuse of funds, the country must take on a loan from the IFS to the tune of $3 billion. It is unavoidable, I'm afraid, Harriet."

"Thank you, President Swish." Harriet turned to the camera. "That was President Janeee Swish there, ladies and gentlemen, speaking from her headquarters in Tokyo Stratis."

Sempre's eyes bulged and a large vein came out on his forehead. His face reddened with anger (you might even have seen it change colour, but for the all the dust that covered it).

"Janeee Swish! Her meddling PASIVs are in control?!" he barked, then looked skyward. "Herra, why do you hate me so? C'mon NITs! Sempre says 'Follow me!'"

Just then, a light rain began to fall. People turned up their collars against the wet stuff and hurried on through the drizzle. Sempre didn't have a coat, the rain just fell on him, washing the soot and dust from out of his clothes and hair. It was like dropping a dirty coin into a can of Earth-based cola, the way that the rain cleaned him up. The NITs snuggled in under his armpits to keep from getting wet, as a trail of brown water followed him wherever he went. More and more of his appearance was being revealed to the Muhaze populace, but it wasn't until he got into the downtown area and stopped at a zebra crossing that he was fully recognised.

A little boy with a baseball cap looked up at him. His mother was busy on her handheld.

"Mummy? Look… It's the president. But he looks all funny."

"*He*?' said his preoccupied mother, "Don't you mean *she*? Don't you mean Janeee Swish, my darling."

"No, not that one. It's the bad president. The ugly one, before Janeee."

Sempre sneered at the boy.

"Mummy! He's making faces at me, mummy! Look!"

The woman turned, obliging her spoilt child. Her bored face quickly turned to one of abject horror.

"David Sempre!" she shrieked. "It's him! He's back from the dead! Everyone, run for your lives!"

The small crowd of people waiting to cross the street erupted into a frenzy of rubbernecking:

"Oh, Herra. She's right!" said one.

"Shizzing Nora. The Sempre's back!" said another.

"Hey, wait, he's shorter than before!" said a third.

"Yeah, and now he's got boobs!" said a fourth.

David Sempre let out his biggest roar yet. It was so loud that he stopped the traffic. Brakes squealed as the NITs flew out from underneath his armpits and hovered, buzzing loudly, waiting for his command, ready to obliterate more innocent life. People began to run in all directions. They screamed and shouted:

"He's still alive!"

"He's disgusting!"

"He's a size 48D!"

And so forth...

In his fury, Sempre resolved, then and there, to find Janeee Swish, kill her, then take control of the city once again.

He knew from the megatron broadcast that her offices were on Tokyo Stratis.

He would go there now.


As Sempre continued his march, the pedestrians became few and far between. Word of his return was spreading like wildfire, and all around shops were being closed and locked, their blinds drawn down and shutters shut. People in cars turned around, making U-turns in the middle of the road, then headed home, where they turned off all their lights, and turned on their TVs. Street-trams stopped and passengers got off, then hurried away into alleyways and dark shadows like Earth-based mice to their holes. Fear transferred itself from person to person, like an electric current through a grid, and soon everyone was touched by the terror of David Sempre's return.

In those little, panic-stricken homes, TV sets flickered with an interrupted newsflash. Ignacio Phinn was in the studio, with a new blonde hairpiece perfectly in place, and his mic held confidently in hand. He began to speak:

"Ladies and gentlemen of Tapi-36. We have just received news that an unnamed individual is on the rampage through the downtown area of our fair city. There is a rumour that this person, if indeed it *is* a person, is none other than Mr. David Sempre, the former president of Tapi-36 and leader of TAPCON. But I must reiterate that this is only a rumour at this point in time, the identity has not been confirmed. So please, good citizens, do not be alarmed. Our forces will soon have everything under control. There is no need to worry unduly."

Phinn pressed his earpiece in his left ear and looked down at the floor to concentrate. News was coming in: "Wait... yes... I've just been told that we have some live pictures from Sashan Avenue. Great news!"

Phinn loved the drama of real-time reporting; being live on air while the events were unfolding nearby. He thought it made him look good, dealing with these kind of stories; improvising his way through a dangerous situation; keeping cool and unflustered. It made him feel important; like a TV big-shot.

*A big-time, prime time, big-shot. Yeah, that's what I am,* he said to himself. The problem was, Phinn was rubbish at this sort of thing. He always said the most banal stuff when under pressure.

He turned to the screen behind him. It was an aerial shot from a helicopter flying over the Muhaze Central Shuttle Station and banking left at the old Sports Stadium. The pictures from the chopper showed the craft winding down Sashan Avenue, while underneath shoppers were running in the opposite direction and screaming.

Pandemonium had broken out. People were getting trampled. Sirens started to sound. *But, at least the rain has stopped,* thought Phinn, more concerned about his toupée. He then realised it would be best not to say that out loud, so instead, he thought of something else: "Ooof," began Phinn, "that looks a bit, um, unsafe."

Off camera, Harriet Honeste grimaced at Phinn's hokum. She made her way into the producer's studio.

Tristan Hughes-Kitsch was directing the show like a headless chicken. He turned as Harriet slammed the door behind her and said: "Tristan, you've no choice but to send me in. Phinn's hopeless!

Tristan didn't need much encouragement. He tilted back his beret on his head and sat back in his Director's chair, the one with his name on the back.

"OK, Harriet, you're on, darling." Then shouted: "Make-up? Fill those cracks!"

Harriet looked to the heavens.

Back in the studio, the screen showed that the Heli-

Cam had found Sempre. He was still marching down the street, but now he was the only person in view. The streets were completely deserted. Sempre paused to look up at the hovering copter and waved his arms above his head and roared at it. The camera pulled in close. Sempre's face was torn with the agony of his predicament. His hands clawed at his body with a renewed sense of disgust. He thundered at the chopper. "Go away!" he shouted. "Leave me alone!"

"Eeew," managed Phinn. "He looks like... an old woman."

"And what's wrong with that, Ignacio?" pronounced Harriet Honeste, walking into view, as the camera came back to the studio.

"Ah, Harriet," began Phinn. "I see you've come to join us. What an honour to have your company on this fine morning. Well, I mean, weather wise, um, except for the rain, that is."

"Yes, quite," she replied. *What a numbskull.* She turned to the camera, her teeth gleaming like so many millions of stars surrounding a black hole. "Citizens of Muhaze, I would ask that everyone remain calm during these troubling times. And please, stay at home until this situation is taken care of. I am sure that normal service will resume shortly. In the meantime, stay tuned for more live pictures. We'll be back after this break, when Kendall Crisp will be reporting live from the scene." Harriet beamed a smile that said: 'That's how you do off-the-cuff reporting. Read 'em and weep, Ignacio.'

The screens of Tapi-36 then flashed to a commercial advertising the new anti-gravity car while, in the studio, Harriet berated Phinn.

"You bumbling old goon," she began. "Can't you get anything right?"

"Well, I... um -"

"Don't blow this, Phinn. This is a big story. Stay out of my way. Got me?"

Through their earpieces Tristan counted down... "and we're back in 5, 4, 3, 2, 1... Go, Harriet!"

Phinn sulked as Harriet continued: "Welcome back, Muhaze. A late breaking piece... We have Dr. Tamashito from the Mu-U on the line. Good morning, Doctor.

Thank you for joining us."

A picture of Dr. Tamashito came on screen with his name underneath, and his voice was heard on the telephone connect: "It's my pleasure, Harriet."

"Thank you, Doctor. Now, you've no doubt seen the images, those horrific images on our screens this morning, can you tell us: What's going on? Who is this? Is it David Sempre?"

Tamashito began slowly. "Yes, it would appear to me that this is indeed David Sempre. But somehow it would seem that he has been *altered* in some fashion, possibly by augmentation implants - it is very difficult to say. He is shorter than before and appears to have a more 'feminine' torso. I have looked closely at the images and can see that there is a ring off stitches around the neck area, which tells me that some sort of grafting has taken place."

"Grafting?" asked Harriet. "You mean…?"

"Yes, I do. His head has been grafted onto a different body. Grafting is a technique we have used for some time now. But only in small mammals. It is only recently that the knowledge has appeared to enable us to graft heads onto bodies of humans."

"Heads onto bodies?" said Phinn. "You mean actually putting a head on another body?"

Harriet rolled her eyes.

"Yes, Ignacio. Precisely that," replied Tamashito, patiently.

"So," continued Harriet, "it is your guess that David Sempre has somehow survived the destruction of TAPCON Towers and then *someone* has done this to our former President?"

"That is correct," answered Tamashito.

"But who? Who would do such an abominable thing?"

"A good question, Harriet. And my instinct would tell me that this is the work of The Specialists. The scientists working for TAPCON. I was one of them, in my time. Regretfully."

"Yes, your unfortunate story is well known, Doctor. And may I say that you have the continued support of the nation in that matter." Harriet made her 'sincere' face here.

34

"Thank you, Harriet. But I must warn the people of Tapi-36, that Sempre is not our real threat."

"Oh, how so?"

"The bug-like creatures that are flying around him, following him? These are what we should fear the most."

"Why? Why is that, Dr. Tamashito?" asked Phinn.

"Well, those aren't bugs, Ignacio. Those are NITs."

"Oh, I see, he's got nits, has he? Well, I've got some fabulous Earth-based tea-tree oil that will have them cleared up in no time at all."

Harriet was watching her co-host with a sour, pained look.

Tamashito corrected the newsman. "No, not that kind of nit, Ignacio. It's an acronym - N. I. T. - it stands for 'Neurological Interface Technology'."

"Oh, I see," replied Phinn. But he didn't see at all. All he'd heard was: 'sciencey-words-blah-blah-blah-more-sciencey-words' and had switched off his brain.

"And what do these NITs do exactly, Doctor?" asked Harriet.

"Well, these are the same NITs that wiped out the Code's animals on Baal-500. They were developed by TAPCON - by the Specialists. They are deadly. Quick to act. Their prey is killed almost instantly on attack. A total misuse of science, if you ask me."

"How horrible," said Harriet.

"And it would appear that David Sempre has some control over them. They seem to be acting on his command. This is most worrying. Our forces must take extreme care if they are engaging with our former President."

Harriet looked worried at this. She was being told, via her earpiece, to cut the interview short. "Well, thank you, Dr. Tamashito. Thank you for joining us this morning."

Tamashito's picture came off screen and the broadcast cut back to the pair of visibly shaken journos.

A flustered Harriet began. "That was Dr. Tamashito there, from the Mu-U. Well, it would appear that our worst fears have been confirmed. David Sempre has indeed 'returned from the dead'. We'll be back after this break. Til then, stay safe, Muhaze."

More adverts came on the air - Nigel-666's new film,

cheese that had no smell, etc. But out there, in the city, there was a wave of fear seizing hold of the general public. And in her offices overlooking Paradi Square, Janeee Swish sent the new Muhaze Police Force downtown. She also ordered for a Code Red to be put into action: all armed forces to be placed on stand-by.

# Chapter 7
*11:38 - 13 October, 2187 (Muhaze, Tapi-36)*


The street-tram came to a grinding halt. Polo and Kané both looked out of the window, to see what the problem was. People were walking quickly out of town. The traffic had also turned around and it seemed as if the Number 2 tram was the only vehicle heading towards the city centre. And now it too had stopped, outside the old Zip building, home of the new, imaginatively titled, TV network 'Nu-Zip'. The mutant driver up front put on his handbrake, turned the engine off, got out of his seat and left the tram. Not a word was given as an excuse.

Polo turned to Kané: "What the shizz is going on?"

Kané shrugged his shoulders. "I've no idea, Polo. But something's not right."

A young woman sitting at the front suddenly let out a scream. "He's back! He's back!" she yelled, then ran off the bus. The remaining passengers got up and followed her.

"Who's back?" shouted Polo. But it was too late, the woman had gone. "Well, we can't sit here all day, Dr. Rexian will be waiting for you."

"Polo, look, there's obviously something up. Let's go back home and -"

But Polo was already on her feet and heading down the aisle. "No, Kané. C'mon, we'll walk the rest of the way. It's not far, it'll take us ten minutes, tops. We can still make it for noon."

Kané shook his head and followed her. He knew Polo was right. He had to get better. It was for the best, for both of them.

Outside, people were rushing past. Fear showed on every face that went by. Polo and Kané stood motionless as the Muhazians hurried on.

Polo stopped one of them. "What's going on? What's happening?"

"Sempre, he's back!" replied the man, visibly shaken. "David Sempre is back from the dead!"

Polo looked down Sashan Avenue. In the distance she saw a helicopter hovering over Paradi Square. People were pouring out of the east part of the city. Police cars could be heard in the distance, and soon they were in full view. Polo and Kané stood and watched as the cars swung into Sashan Avenue and down the street in the direction of the chopper.

"Oh, wow!" said Kané. "This I have to see!"

"No way, Kané. We're going to Dr. Rex's. It's this way…"

But Kané was gone.

*Fire! Once a thrill-seeker, always a thrill-seeker,* thought Polo. *Drain him!*

Polo followed Kané down the street, protesting as she went, but her cousin was deaf to her.

*This is so cool*, thought Kané, as he reached into his pocket and took out his hand-held. He started taking pictures of the scene around him.

"Kané, c'mon, let's get out of here," said Polo. "This looks dangerous." She reached out to stop him but he shrugged her off.

"No way, Po. I'm not going to miss this. You leave, if you want. I'm staying here."

Polo stopped for a second or two, looked around at the melee, then followed her cousin. "Kané, wait for me!"

The police cars had pulled up at the North-west end of

Paradi Square, at the corner of Centris and Chièvres Stratis. They'd formed a blockade in front of Janeee Swish's presidential offices, and camera crews were taking up their places at various vantage points around the Square. The streets were now empty. The only sound was that of the helicopter in the sky.

Then, it happened.

Sempre turned the corner of Sashan and Algonquin.

He stood there, foaming at the mouth. A tiny ball of unleashed fury. He was panting, taking in the whole of the media frenzy that now surrounded him. The megatron on the north end was showing live pictures, with live sound of the siege.

Sempre roared. "Where is Janeee Swish?"

Silence.

Then the sound of feedback, as Chief of Police, Captain Harvey Milksilk (a bland looking man of average height) began to speak through his megaphone. "Um... Hello, Mr. Sempre, welcome back, sir. How are you today?"

"You what?" shouted Sempre.

"I said: How are you today, sir?"

"Yeah, I know what you said. I just wondered why you were asking me such a stupid question, given the circumstances."

"Um... I... um..."

"Never mind! I want to see Janeee Swish. And I want to see her now!"

The megatron screen cut back to Milksilk. "Yeah, OK. Well, you see, sir. We can't do that right now, because..."

"Why not? I know she's in there."

"Um... well. The thing is... she's, um, she's gone out for a minute or two. So, in the meantime, let's talk."

"No! I don't want to talk to you, you imbecile! I want Janeee Swish!"

"Well, as I said, Mr. Sempre she's -"

Sempre was getting angry. "NITs? Sempre says: 'Kill the bland looking man with the megaphone!'"

The NITs flew out from beside Sempre and swarmed towards the Captain.

"Ummm, right," said the Chief. "OK, OK, I'll get her

now! Call off the NITs! Anything! Please!"

Sempre relented. "NITs? Sempre says; 'Come back'."

The NITs obeyed. Reluctantly.

\*

In the TV studio, Harriet and Phinn watched with all the glee of a pair of necrophiliacs entering a morgue.

\*

As the camera panned back to Sempre it intercut with a view of the people watching the event. It paused for a moment on Polo and Kané's faces, then cut back to the Square.

Unfortunately for Polo, Sempre had caught a glimpse of her on the screen and recognised her immediately.

"Wait! That girl... er, that boy... um, that one there!"

Sempre pointed to the Megatron. The camera scanned through the crowd until it landed again on Polo.

"Yes, her! Send her to me, now! Or I will let my NITs loose - and this time I will show no mercy!"

"But, Mr. Sempre. That is not President Swish. That is... well, that's nobody."

Polo wasn't happy with being called a 'nobody'.

"Excuse me, Mr. Megaphone. I'm not 'nobody", sir. I'm Polo Smith, cousin of Mikita Smith. You know, the person who just so happened to save the entire planet?"

Milksilk was on the ball. "Oh, yes, the weirdo, with the funny, um, 'condition'?"

"Yes, I mean, no! It wasn't a condition," replied Polo, testily, "It was the Golden... Hey, your supposed to support wielders, not poke fun at them!"

"ENOUGH!!" roared Sempre. "Send the girl, boy, whatever, to me. NOW! Or the NITs will kill you ALL!"

Milksilk looked at Polo. "Miss Smith. Would you mind?"

Polo look disgruntled, but nevertheless walked straight out into the Square and over to Sempre. As she neared her captor, she noticed his body for the first time. It was Sempre's head all right, but the rest of it was... a woman's. She saw the join at the neck, the stitches, they looked raw and sore. She'd never seen anything quite like this. Not even the aliens from out of town that came into Voltz 'N' Boltz were this horrible.

As Polo approached, the NITs buzzed louder.

Sempre reassured them. "Calm down, NITs. It's nothing to be scared of." Then to Polo: "So, Miss Smith, we meet again. Where is your sister, the troublemaker? She's not with you today?"

"No, Sempre. She's far, far away from here, if you must know."

"Oh, that is good news. The best news I've had all morning, in fact."

"I can imagine," replied Polo, with a sly grin. "You look like shizz, Sempre, if you don't mind me saying so."

"And so do you. What are you now? A boy or a girl?"

"I could ask you the same question."

"Ah, very good, Miss Smith. Yes, you see, I have been taken advantage of, so to speak. A scientific joke, I feel. But this is what I am now, I don't have to like it. And anyway, as soon as I get back what is mine, I'll be able to fix it so I can have a different body. And this time it'll be a tall one!"

The NITs hummed loudly at Sempre's state of anxiety.

"Be calm, my NITs. Be calm. Plenty time for that later."

"What's going on over there?" It was Milksilk on his megaphone. "What are you two talking about?"

"Nothing that concerns you, Chief!" replied Sempre. He grabbed Polo around the neck and held her in front of him. "Now. Get me Janeee Swish. I want to speak to her. Or this one gets the NITs treatment."

Polo watched as the police mumbled something to each other. She saw a cameraman go into the offices with an officer.

Milksilk came on again: "I'm sending a camera in right now. You can talk to her on the megatron."

Sempre weighed up the offer. "OK. That'll do!"

Sempre was squeezing Polo's neck too tightly, she was slowly turning purple.

"Hey, watch it, Sempre," said Polo.

"Don't worry, Miss Smith. You will come to no harm, as long as you do what I say. My quarrel is not with you."

Clearly, Sempre's female side was coming to the fore; his mother's hormones were influencing him - though she had been quite a manly woman, so the effect was minimal.

Captain Harvey had hooked-up his Heath-Robinson ham-radio. "OK, Mr. Sempre. We have the President onscreen now."

"President, my bahookie," muttered Sempre, under his breath.

Suddenly, a droid flew out from a Police van. Sempre watched it warily as it flew towards himself and Polo.

"No need to worry, Mr. Sempre. The droid will pick up your voice and relay it to Miss Swish. No cause for concern, just speak clearly, sir."

"This guy is making me wish I hadn't got up this morning," said Sempre.

"What was that, Mr. Sempre?" asked Milksilk. "We didn't pick that up, speak more clearly, if you would, please."

"I said: I wish you would turn off your megaphone so I wouldn't have to listen to your voice."

"Oh, right," managed Milksilk. "OK, Mr. Sempre, here's President Swish now."

Janeee Swish appeared on the megatron screen. She looked calm. This was her first 'incident' as President and she wanted to handle it well.

"Good afternoon, Mr. Sempre," she began. "And how may we help you today, sir?"

"How may you help me?" he replied.

"Yes, what can I do for you, sir?"

"Well, you could try dying for starters."

Janeee looked confused. "I don't understand, Mr. Sempre."

"No, I guess you wouldn't. Look, here's what's going to happen. You will immediately vacate your office... sorry, my office, and I will walk in there, sit in your seat and recommence doing the job that I'm still entitled to do."

"That's not possible, Mr. Sempre. You see, we had an election and -"

"Yes, yes, so I hear. But, tell me Miss. Swish, why did you have an election?"

"Well, because you were dead, Mr. Sempre."

"But I am *not* dead, am I? I'm right here, alive and well. So, the election is null and void. I'm *still* alive, therefore I'm *still* President."

Janeee's brow furrowed. "But Mr. Sempre, the election was officially ratified by the IFS. TAPCON is no more, sir. I'm afraid you'll have to -"

"I'm afraid I'll have to kill this girl/boy thing right here!"

Janeee look perturbed. "Mr. Sempre. Please. Let us work something out between us."

"There is nothing to work out! Either you give me back my job or Polo Smith gets the nasty NITs! What will it be, *President* Swish?"

Janeee didn't know what to do. She hadn't planned on this happening, not in a million years. She was new at her job and inexperienced. Full of confidence and worthy ideals, yes, but a hostage situation? With a total psychotic? She hadn't even had time to assemble advisors. The Chief of Police was down by the Square, she couldn't very well ask him for advice. She had to do this herself. There was a young woman's life at stake here. But what could she say? What could she do? Then she thought of something...

"OK," she began. "You can have your job back."

Sempre's mouth dropped open. "What? Really?"

All eyes turned to the megatron in stunned silence.

"Yes, Mr. Sempre." She got up out of her seat. "Look. Here. My chair is empty. It's all yours. Captain Milksilk? Tell your men to put down their weapons."

Milksilk's brow wrinkled in incredulity. "But President. Surely you can't mean to -"

"Do as I say, Captain."

The Captain shrugged his shoulders. "OK, men. You heard the President, weapons down."

The policemen tossed their guns and blasters to the ground.

Sempre laughed. Then stopped suddenly.

*A trick! It must be. Why would she do this? It's completely ridiculous!* He thought.

"No, wait," he said. "I have a better idea."

Janeee sat back down in her chair. "Yes, Mr. Sempre?

Please continue."

"I want that helicopter." He pointed to the one hovering high above the square. "And I want it to take me to an augmentation laboratory, the one in Grafuulen."

"But Mr. Sempre, there are no augmentation laboratories on Tapi-36, they've all been banned for years," replied Janeee.

"Ha! Ha! Ha! That's what YOU think, Miss Swish. Where do you think the Scientists worked before working for me? Mitchell and Quince? They were the best Aug merchants this side of the Michael-6 Quadrant. Until I killed them this morning, that is."

Janeee looked shocked. "Killed them? Mr. Sempre, I must warn you that as a war criminal you are entitled to a fair trial, and any admission of guilt in such a public arena will only do you a mis-service. Please, Why don't you come into the building and we can talk this through."

Sempre's bottom lip stuck out. "NO! I want the helicopter! NOW!"

The NITs buzzed loudly. There were getting antsy. Or rather - 'nitty'.    Sempre's hold on Polo tightened again. "Not so rough!" she protested.

"Oh, pardon me, Miss Smith," he replied, loosening his grip. "My hormones are all over the place today."

There was a further silence across the square, but soon Janeee spoke.

"Very well, Mr. Sempre. We will bring the helicopter down into Paradi Square. Chief Milksilk? Clear the area."

Milksilk shook his head, and signaled his men to proceed.

## Chapter 8

*11:49 - 13 October, 2187 (Starship Krashaon, Michael 6 Quadrant)*

Mikita could tell Zanthu was worried.

"Mikita, we have to get out of here."

"Wait, Zanthu, what do you mean? Calm down. Tell me what's happened."

"The Elders have decreed that we are not to marry because of your wielding the Golden Circuit - that your people are to blame for the animal slaughters. *And* I'm to be sent to the seminary for a <u>year.</u> The only thing left is for us is to leave."

"What? But how? Where can we go?"

"I don't know yet, Mikita. All I know is that I love you, and I will never leave you."

"Oh, Zanthu. I feel the same, but surely - your people - they <u>must</u> come first?"

"Drain my people! They are idiots. Fools! If only my father was alive, he would see through all of this. He married my mother and she was the one with the gift of wielding in her bloodline. He must have known the dangers. No, Mikita. We have no choice. We will leave the ship. I know of a small craft. The Yagar-34. It was my father's. One that he would use for his personal missions. I went on it several times. I've flown it, in fact. It's not used anymore. It's down on P Deck."

"But they'll not allow you to get anywhere near it,

Zanthu. There's no way they'll allow that."

"They might not let me, Mikita. But they'll let Leylaan."

"OK. So supposing he can get us onboard somehow, then what? Where do we go after that?"

"I don't know. I'll figure it out, don't worry. The closest planet that we know, I guess. Cratchen-404 is nearby. It's hospitable, I hear. We'll hide there until I can think this through. I'll go talk to Leylaan now. You stay here. Don't answer the door, OK?"

"Yes, Zanthu, of course. Please be careful."

Zanthu nodded, kissed Mikita, then left to find his brother.


So much had happened to Mikita recently. She had gone from being a person lost to a person found. Yet still, everywhere she went, things went wrong. She knew it was the fault of the Golden Circuit; it was a curse to her even now. After all the time she had spent with the Guardians learning to control it, work it, tap into its great potential, she was still left with the fall-out of its after-effects. There was a high price to pay for being a wielder. And now, after only a few weeks of being with the Codes she had already alienated them. Through no fault of her own. It was all to do with the GC.

There was another thing. Something else was bothering her. Something that she didn't want to address at this time. Her relationship with Zanthu. She couldn't help it, but she was feeling trapped. She'd been a loner all her life, someone who avoided long-term relationships, and now, here she was, almost married - and to someone she'd only known for a few months. Part of her wanted to run away, the other part wanted the complete opposite. She loved Zanthu, she knew that, but his love was total, all-consuming, faultless. Hers, well, it was different, more hesitant, more questioning. Hers lacked the confidence that Zanthu's love had. Perhaps it would come in time. But then, perhaps it wouldn't...

Marta came to her, sensing that her master was troubled. The little muidog was right, of course. She could read Mikita like a book.

"Am I that transparent, Marta? That you can so easily feel my moods? You are so clever. Oh, I wish you could speak, and let me know what I should do."

Marta gave a little bark.

Mikita smiled. "What was that? An answer to my problems?"

Marta barked again.

"Clever girl. Come here."

Mikita reached out to the puppy and she scampered into her arms. "You know me so well, why can't everyone else see my like you do?"

A knock at the door.

Zanthu.

"It is settled. We leave in an hour. I will come for you. Until then, Mikita…"

Mikita nodded. "OK, Zanthu. If that is what you wish?"

"It is," he replied. Then ducked back out into the corridor.

*That's settled then,* said Mikita, dryly, to herself.

She looked over to her Marcie-held, and thought to try Polo once more.

*Oh, there is no point. What would I say? Yeah sorry, Polo, it's all gone wrong and now I'm escaping with Zanthu to Herra knows where?*

That was a bad idea. Polo would only worry about her. She would try her again, when things were safer.

Whenever that would be…

## Chapter 9
*11:58 - 13 October, 2187 (Starship Argon, Lumiol-S3 Apex, Michael 6 Quadrant)*

Spalding was dressed as he always dressed. Dark navy suit, white shirt, pink tie, highly-polished black shoes and a briefcase in his right hand - chained to his wrist. He wore rimless glasses and his face had a slightly pinched demeanour, like there was a bad smell in the room that constantly irritated him. His hair was thinning on top, but he combed over what there was in an effort to hide his baldness - Spalding's vanity was there for all to see, but he didn't care a jot what people thought of him. He ducked through the connecting docking shaft and out into the Loading Bay. Jameson and McGilvary were there to meet him.

"Welcome, Reg," said Jameson, extending his hand. "Great to see you."

"Cut the horse shizz, Jameson," replied Spalding, ignoring his pleasantry. "You don't want me here, and I don't want to be here - so let's just get this over with as quickly and as painlessly as possible, and then I can go back to my day job. What do you say?"

"Ah, you've not changed a bit," replied Jameson.

Spalding read the Captain's sarcasm. "Very good, Jameson. Very amusing. Now let's get started."

"Would you like to be shown your quarters first, Reg? Freshen up a bit before we start? Lieutenant McGilvary here will escort you -"

"No, later, Jameson. Time is money."

Jameson nodded to McGilvary. "Thank you, Corporal," he said. "That is all."

McGilvary replied with a brief "Yes, sir." And left.

Spalding watched the corporal leave. He peered over his rimless glasses as McGilvary went thru the door and it automatically shut behind her. "She's very obedient, Jameson. Is she like that after hours, too?"

Jameson closed his eyes and shook his head in disgust at Spalding's comment.

Spalding grinned at the Captain's reaction, then moved to a nearby surface and put down the briefcase he was carrying. He pressed in some code on a display near the handle and the lid opened with a soft, mechanical whirr and impressively smooth action. Spalding turned and gave Jameson a look that said 'I only use the best equipment', then took out a small Furtzwang Video Book-AV31. A new portable device used for meeting briefings. He put it on the table then said: "Meeting 562.90 - Argon. Captain Phil Jameson and Mr. Reg Spalding present." The device switched itself on and a hologram appeared in mid-air, approximately 1m x 2m.

Jameson had to concede. "Nice bit of kit, Spalding."

"You bet. Now be a good boy and watch the video."

The hologram sequence began with a new IFS logo and a voiceover that began to detail the plans for the next Time Stretch. It was full of hyperbole, images of space craft, IFS crews helping other alien races, flags being planted on barren planets, astronauts shaking hands with smiling aliens etc., etc. All very pro-IFS. The effect of the propaganda was impressive. After two minutes, it came to an end.

Jameson looked quizzically at his counterpart. "Why are you showing me this, Spalding? This is just for the tourists, surely?"

"Samms wanted you to see it, Jameson. He wanted me to remind you who you were working for." Spalding exhaled impatiently. "He thinks you're a loose canon. He wants me to assure him that you'll bring this project in on time, with no fuss. Do you think I'll be able to report back with a positive, Philip?"

Jameson looked peeved. He hated it when Spalding called him 'Philip'. He bit his tongue. "Of course, Reg. No problem at my end. Absolutely."

"Good. That's the right answer."

*

"Your uniform looks great," said Tora to Newton.

Newton blushed. "Aw, thanks Tora. Yours does, too."

Tora smiled.

"Right, lovebirds," said Marcie. "Can someone give me a hand with this tie? I've never worn one before."

"I'll show you," said Linden. "It's really rather easy."

"Thanks, Linden."

The door to the Peers quarters slid open. In came Dr. Gössner, with Reg Spalding.

"Peers, may I introduce to you Mr. Reginald Spalding. He is here from the IFS to oversee the ceremony."

The Peers fell into line, just as they had done when Mikita first landed on Plaateux-5.

"Ah, such discipline," remarked Spalding. "What a pleasure to see you all. What an honour. Let first say how delighted I am to meet you, and how proud the IFS is to have you with us, as our new ambassadors to the cosmos. I am sure our working relationship will be most productive in all areas and zones."

Spalding didn't have a clue how to talk to anyone below the age of twenty. The Peers recognised this instantly. Ellery couldn't resist having a dig at him.

"What are the perks, Mr. Spalding? Of the job, I mean?"

"Ellery!" exclaimed Tina. "Don't be so impertinent."

Spalding held up a hand. "No, Dr. Gössner, please, allow me to answer the question." He walked slowly over to stand in front of the boy, and fixed him with a gaze that made Ellery feel quite uncomfortable.

"The perks? Well, Mr. Greyslate. For a start, you get to work for the IFS. What a privilege for someone so young, don't you agree?"

Ellery nodded. He found he couldn't speak, such was

50

Spalding's stare.

"Secondly, you get to travel the universe as our ambassadors. A joy, I would have thought?"

Ellery nodded again.

"And thirdly, and most importantly, you remain alive."

Ellery's eyes widened. He didn't understand. *Alive?* He said nothing in reply.

"I'm joking!" said Spalding, laughing. "You should see your face, Mr. Greyslate."

The other Peers joined the laughter, out of nervousness more than anything else. It subsided quickly and the room was left in an embarrassing silence.

Spalding was still staring at Ellery, as Dr. Gössner spoke: "Well, thank you for that, Mr. Spalding. Now, I will take you to the Stateroom - if you please?" Tina gestured to the door.

"Yes, of course, Dr. Gössner. How kind." He turned to the Peers. "So nice to meet you all." He smiled, creepily, and left with Tina.

After he'd gone, the Peers looked at each other.

"Don't like him," said Tora.

"Yeah, and what's with the hair?" said Marcie.

# Chapter 10
*12:03 - 13 October, 2187 (Muhaze, Tapi-36)*

Sempre bundled the pilot and cameraman out of the chopper and pushed Polo in in front of him. Keeping a watchful eye on the Police, he stepped up into the cockpit, the NITs staying close at his side. He turned to Polo, green ooze weeping from the stitches at his neck. "Do you know how to fly a helicopter, Miss Smith?"

Polo looked to the heavens. "Oh yeah, sure," she said, sarcastically. "I have my own private one that I fly to my work at Voltz 'N' Boltz. For fire's sake, of course I don't know how to fly one!"

Sempre looked slightly perturbed. "Hmmm. Well, that is a problem... because neither do I."

Polo sighed in disgust.

Sempre carried on: "But, how difficult can it be?" he said, taking hold of the control sticks and pulling them back.

The helicopter made a sudden surging noise as the nose shot up rapidly in front. They heard a bump at the rear as the tail-rotor hit the tarmac.

"Hey, take it easy," said Polo. "Less throttle and more brake, or you'll get us both killed."

Sempre grinned a devilish grin and began to laugh, his

female body parts jiggling about as he did so. He pushed down on the throttle and sent the chopper careering towards the buildings of Chièvres Stratis.

"Oh, shizzing Herra!" cried Polo, reaching out for something to hang on to.

The Ex-TAPCON boss was still laughing as he leaned back into his chair pulling hard on the controls. He didn't seem to care whether they crashed or not. Down below, the entire Police Force scattered itself in all directions.

Polo began to scream.

"Don't worry, Miss Smith. I've got this," said Sempre, as the chopper barely scraped over the top of the buildings and shot northward towards the Muhaze Shuttle Station.

"There," began Sempre, "Now the only problem will be landing this thing, but we'll cross that bridge when we come to it."

"Oh, goody," Polo replied. "I can't wait for that."

\*

Harry Milksilk made his way from Paradi Square up to Janeee Swish's office.

"President Swish, I have ordered my men to tail the chopper. But I need to have your permission to shoot and ask questions later. Do I have that, ma'am?"

Janeee shook her head. "No. No you do not, Captain Milksilk."

"But President Swish, Sempre is heavily armed - those NITs - we have received reports from the Airfield that they have already brutally murdered several workers and guards. We must take no chances. And the people are panicking. And we know what happened last time they did that."

Milksilk was referring to the looting after the last Froome attack.

Janeee paused for a moment and was about to agree to Milksilk's demands, then saw sense. "No. I must stand firm on this matter. We bring him in unharmed."

Milksilk nodded. "Very well, President Swish. As you wish."

"Thank you, Captain. Now, let's get this sorted, and remember - he has a hostage."

*

Sempre was managing to keep the chopper from crashing into various tall buildings on the way out of Muhaze, and he breathed a distinctly feminine sigh of relief when they'd reached the outlying land to the north of the city.

He felt Polo's eyes on him.

"Do I look so very ugly to you, Miss Smith?"

Polo was surprised by this question. Sempre appeared full of self-pity. She was amazed that a man who once had so much personal power could be such a sad individual. Admittedly a crazy one, but so sad on the inside.

"Um… well… yes, you do, Sempre. You look draining awful."

"Yes, I suppose so," he replied, turning to look out of the cockpit window. The NITs were quiet and had stopped buzzing, they nested calmly under his arms.

"But you'll get a couple Augs and that'll be you sorted out. Don't worry, Mr. Sempre."

Polo was trying to keep him calm with her chat. She thought this to be the best idea, seeing as how she was 500 feet above ground, and a madman was at the wheel.

But Sempre's eyes unexpectedly flashed with anger. "Yes, then I'll come back to Muhaze and destroy Tamashito and Janeee Swish! I will crush them like so much dust!"

*Oh well,* thought Polo, *I tried.*

Across the desolate terrain of the planet, Grafuulen loomed in the distance. The second city of Tapi-36 was much smaller than Muhaze, not as developed as the capital, and without the swagger of its larger neighbour - like a younger brother, but with acne, and a limp.

Polo attempted more conversation. "So, this Augs place, where is it exactly?"

"Downtown. On Klingdorfer Street."

*Klingdorfer Street…* thought Polo. *That sounds familiar…*

Sempre continued. "We'll need to land this thing

somewhere close by. And I'm going need a disguise of some sort."

Sempre looked at Polo's hat. "Give me that hat... In fact, give me all of your clothes. You can have my mother's dress."

Polo looked horrified.

Sempre shook his head. "If you want to stay alive you'll give me your suit, Miss Smith."

The NITs hummed threateningly under his arms.

"Oh, great. I finally find my look and a lunatic takes it from me. What the shizz is going on in my life!"

"Temper, temper, Miss Smith. Anger won't solve anything." Sempre laughed at his joke. Actually, he thought anger solved *everything*. He'd been taught that by his mother and father since he was a child. It was what drove him to do the things he did. It's what got him up in the morning, and sent him to sleep at night. His whole life had revolved around it.

As the helicopter approached central Grafuulen, Polo noticed a low building with a large, flat roof.

"There, Sempre. That building over there. Looks like a good place to land."

"Well-spotted, Miss Smith. You're cleverer than you look."

"Oh, thanks," she replied, sarcastically. Then shook her head.

Sempre banked the helicopter to the East, then down towards the roof of the building. He'd quickly mastered the combination of rotor and cyclic sticks, and was feeling very confident that he could make a good landing. But confidence is one thing - over-confidence another, and Sempre found himself coming in far too fast.

"Watch out, Sempre!" exclaimed Polo. "You're too hot on the controls!"

But it was too late.

As the chopper hit the roof there was an almighty thump that rocked the two of them to their respective cores. Sempre bore the worst of the hit, his head coming down onto the stick and then whipping back onto the headrest.

Polo was dazed, her seatbelt had saved her from the worst. She looked over at Sempre. He was out cold, his eyes were shut and his head hung limp.

Finding an opportunity to escape had occupied her mind since take-off - this was her chance to make a run for it.

Polo tried to unfasten her seatbelt, but it wouldn't unlock. She tried the door on her side. Nothing. Some overall safety device was obviously in play. Probably due to the crash. Polo cursed her luck.

To her left, Sempre groggily came to. "Oh, my head," he said, shaking it from side to side. His stitches pranged and he yollered like an Earth-based bear with a thorn in its toe. "Shizzing Nora! I've really got to get these staples sorted out!"

Sempre tried his belt, realised that it was stuck, then surveyed the dashboard. A red light was flashing. He decided to press it. There was a loud beep and then the belts unfastened themselves and the doors clicked open. Sempre nodded in appreciation of the design.

"Very nice," he said, then turned to Polo, with a grin. "C'mon, Miss Smith, it's time to get me Augmented."

## Chapter 11
*12:25 - 13 October, 2187 (Muhaze, Tapi-36)*


Gompi and Charly watched the live scenes from Paradi Square on their living room TV - both of them glued to the screen. Sempre's siege was taking place just a few blocks away from their flat in Weah Stratis, down the road from the Weah Mansions, where Gompi used to work for Mr. Dontai.

Both Gompi and Charly agreed that the situation was particularly worrying for them because the couple had only that morning put in their order at the Repro-Life Clinic for a little Gompi. They had decided the time was right to start a family. But the scenes on the TV made them think twice about whether it would be a good idea to bring a child into the world.

"I not like this, Charly," said Gompi. "This very bad news."

"Yes, Gompi," replied Charly. "It very bad."

"We have little Gompi soon, what kind of world we bring him into? Not good one, that for sure."

"No, not good one."

"What we do?"

"I don't know."

"We go and help?"

"How?"

"Let's think."

"Yes, let's."

So Gompi and Charly sat for a bit - just thinking. Then, after a while, Charly said: "I have idea!"

"Oh, that great!" said Gompi. "Tell me what is."

"OK, we both say Tapi-36 not good place, yes?"

Gompi nodded. "Yes. Always things go wrong. Bad people in charge is main cause."

"Yes. But Janeee Swish is nice lady. Clever and kind, yes?"

"Yes, Charly. She very perfect lady. But what your idea?"

"She need help. Help from us mutants. So, we go to Dr. Tamashito. We get him to update mutants on computer. Then we help President Janeee. We help her catch Mr. Sempre and make planet safe for little Gompi when he come."

"Oh, that good, Charly. I like plan. You so smart." Gompi smiled at Charly and she blushed a bit.

"So, Gompi. We go now?"

"Yes, we get bus to Mu-U. We ask at desk for appointment. It be fine. Dr. Tamashito know me. He help us for sure."

Charly nodded her head and got up from her chair. "Let's go, then. Before it too late!"

*

"I'm not sure I want to be an ambassador for the IFS," said Tora.

"Yeah, I know what you mean," replied Marcie. "I want to go back to my old life, before the Guardians, and all of that. I want to be normal again."

Cy disagreed. "Nope. I think it's going to be great. Travelling in all the best starships, visiting planets you've never even heard of. Aliens, weird creatures, it's going to be the best. Isn't it Newton?"

Newton was polishing his shoes. "Definitely, Cy. The best." Newton said the words, but didn't sound convinced. Cy was his best friend, so he couldn't side with the girls on this one.

"Linden, what do you think?" asked Tora.

Linden pushed his specs. His answer was short and non-committal. "I think that we shall see how things go."

"And if things don't go well?" asked Marcie.

"Then we will have to think of a plan."

"A plan?" asked Cy. "What do you mean?"

Linden brought his hands up like he was about to pray. "All our lives we have been told that the GC is dangerous, be careful, don't tell anybody about it. And then, after doing that for all these years, we end up with the Guardians. They only wanted us for the power that we can create as a group. They wanted to harness that for evil purposes. And now the IFS is in control of us. How did we let that happen? It just <u>has</u>. No, I'm tired of being used. I agree with Marcie. I want to go back to being normal, too. There's only one thing: How can we, when we are not normal? We are wielders. And will always be looked upon with suspicion. It is a part of us that we can never be rid of. Not ever."

The others had never seen Linden so downcast.

"Unless there <u>is</u> a way to get rid of it?" said Ellery. "From inside, somewhere. Maybe when we see the source in Sanctuary."

The Peers looked at one another. No one had ever thought of that before.

"We should try it!" exclaimed Tora.

"But we can't use the GC here on the spacecraft," said Marcie. "Dr. Gössner said so."

Linden smiled, then said: "But it's like an Earth-based no-smoking sign."

"What do you mean, Linden?" asked Ellery.

"I mean, it's just a thing. They may ask you to put out your cigarette later, but they can't stop you from lighting it up. Get me?"

"Linden's right," said Marcie. "If we get caught, what are they going to do? Kill us?"

"Well, I'm in," said Tora.

"Me too," said Ellery.

"And me," joined Newton.

Cy was the only one left. He looked upset. He so wanted to travel about in massive spacecraft and wear an IFS uniform.

"Cy?" asked Marcie, "Are you with us?"

The boy looked at the floor.

"Take your time, Cy," said Linden. "There is no rush. We must all be in accordance for this to work. If one of us is against it then we simply won't do it. We have always been a team, that won't change. OK, Cy?"

Cy nodded. "Thanks, Linden."

"It's OK, Cy. You are like a brother to me. You are all like family to me. In fact, more than family."

The Peers smiled. They all felt the same way about each other. Their bond was deep. Their experiences on Plaateux-5 had made that come to pass. They knew each other inside out and outside in. It was something no one could ever take away from them. But their bond to the GC itself had taken its toll. They were tired of carrying the burden of its power. They had seen the chaos it caused, the lives in broke asunder with its force. Now it was time to take back their lives.

# Chapter 12
*12:53 - 13 October, 2187 (Muhaze, Tapi-36)*

After the scene at Paradi Square, Kané had gone home to try and find the last Nanoloxetin tablet. He was in a fevered state - withdrawal was coming on.

Kané cursed Polo. *She's probably flushed them down the toilet... or put them in the garbage!*

Kané's eyes lit up. He immediately went to the trash and emptied the contents out onto the floor. He searched through the cans and rotting vegetables, but found nothing.

Another pang of withdrawal hit him. They would come more regularly now. He needed to do something fast, even if it meant going back on promises he'd made to himself.

He went into Polo's room. Everything in her room was tidied up and neatly put away. Not that Polo was a neat freak; the drawers weren't labelled or anything, it was simply a reflection of how Polo wanted to live - now. Truthfully, honestly, true to herself, like Mikita had encouraged her to. Polo had an inner self-belief that Kané didn't have and it made him jealous. In fact, a lot of things in life made Kané jealous. People that still had their parents, for example. People who didn't have to lie all the time. People who didn't have to puff themselves up with falsehoods and denial. It was why he still resorted to the Nans. Sure, he could blame TAPCON for putting him on the red and white drops in the first place, but that was a long time ago and it had been up to *him* to kick his habit all these years - and he'd still not done it.

He opened Polo's bedside drawer.

Inside it were some of her father's possessions Polo had found when going through Ichiro's clothes at Fizz's. A pipe, some cufflinks, but nothing there of any great value. Then, at the back of the drawer he found a box. It was made of black onyx - regarded as a rare precious stone on Tapi-36. Its healing powers were widely known and such boxes were highly covetable.

*Oh, yes! Good old Po,* thought Kané. *This is worth at least 100 bucks.*

He found the hinge catch on the side of the box and the lid flipped open.

The object inside shone on Kané's face, making him look like a handsome king of Earth-based Egypt.

It was a watch. A old watch. In its original box.

Through the plastic packaging, Kané could see that it was made of gold, with a chain and fob for the waistcoat. At the centre of the dial was a cartoon figure. A mouse, in red shorts and yellow boots, with two big ears and an inane grin on its face. The arms were extended with white-gloved hands pointing an index finger to the hours and minutes notated in Roman numerals around the perimeter of the circle of time.

Kané, shrugged his shoulders and put the watch back into the box.

*Might be worth a few bucks...*

He grabbed his coat and made his way down to the street.


The people of Muhaze were gradually appearing from the safety of their houses. They'd all seen or heard the news. Sempre was gone, in a helicopter with a girl in a man's suit. President Janeee would sort it out. She'd said so. It wasn't their concern anymore.

Kané went to his local pawn shop: 'Keith's Used and Collectables'.

It was shut.

"Shizz it!" he said, out loud.

A woman passing by with a young girl gave him a look. Kané smiled back, embarrassed. He turned to the shop and peered in through the window.

He saw Keith inside, he was watching the TV in his little room at the back. He was a fat, greasy character, with shoulder-length hair, who liked to eat constantly. He was always snacking on something. Usually cheese and onion flavoured chips or Floreato's, the 9oz bag.

"Keith!" shouted Kané, knocking on the window. "It's me, Kané!"

Keith turned at the knock, saw Kané and waved him off, then went back to eating.

"Keith! Open up! I've got something!"

Keith looked round again, annoyed. He shook his head. "Go away, Kané! I'm closed!"

Kané checked the street for the all clear, then reached into his pocket and pulled out the onyx box. He held it up to the window. "Hey, Keith! Look at this!"

Keith shook his head, put down his bag of crisps and made to close the door of his gaff. He was still shaking his head at Kané when he saw the box. He did a quick double take, and then his eyes ballooned like a boil ready to burst.

He was over to the front door of the shop like a rat to fresh garbage bags.

He unlocked the padlock and flung open the front door, checking the street as he did so. There was no one around.

"Kané, how are you, my boy. Still handsome, I see." Keith was the type to use flattery to excess when he wanted something. 'Greasing the sticky wheels of business', he called it.

"Yeah, save it for the judge, Keith."

"Yes, of course, Kané, my son. Of course."

Ushering Kané into his store, Keith rushed behind his counter and turned on the lamp he used for examining things, then got out his magnifying eye-piece. A bead of perspiration broke out on his forehead. It had been years, eleven to be exact, since he'd had a black onyx box in his shop.

"Now, how can I be of assistance to you this fine day,

Kané. How can I help?" he said, leering over the counter.

"I've got this box, with a watch inside. Some kind of Earth-based rodent on it, I dunno. Look, I need a quick sale."

"Let me see, Kané. Let old Keith have a look." Keith held out his hands. His palms already had little pools of sweat gathering on them.

Kané gave him the box.

Keith set in down on the counter and brought his flexi-lamp in closer. He put on his magnifying lens and sat down on his well-worn stool to better study the object. After about 30 seconds of silence examining the box exterior, Keith opened the lid and saw the watch.

*Herra strike me down!* he said to himself.

Keith hoped Kané hadn't sensed his reaction.

He looked up from beneath his flexi-lamp. "Um... Where did you get this, Kané?" he asked, as coolly as he could.

"Why? What does it matter, Keith? C'mon, I need some cash for it. How much can you give me."

Keith sensed a fidgetiness about Kané's demeanour. He knew Kané well enough to work out that he was after money for drugs. He saw enough people in similar circumstances to know the telltale signs. Keith also knew that black onyx could fetch a huge price with the right buyer, or in the right auction. But the watch! It was unheard of to find an item so rare anywhere but on Earth. This was a real find for a small-time pawn merchant. He tried to act normal, despite his fat-encased heart spluttering away inside his chest like a fish on dry land.

"Sure, Kané. No problem. It's just that I wondered if there were anymore like these? You know, from wherever you found this one."

Kané was growing impatient. "No, that's the only one. Now, how much, Keith? I'm in a rush."

Keith paused and looked at the box again. He breathed out a long sigh as if to say 'not sure these can be moved on'. "$50 for the box. $10 for the watch. That's my best offer."

Kané made to gather up the items from the counter. "You think I'm stupid, don't you, Keith. C'mon, we both know this stuff is worth more than that. Don't insult me."

Keith put a slippery palm on top of Kané's hand. "OK, OK, Kané. $100 for the box, $50 for the watch. Take it or leave it."

Kané nodded. "Done. Now, give me the cash. And hurry it up, will you?"

Keith's lips began to move in such a slippery and satisfied way you'd have thought he'd dined out on greasy eels.

## Chapter 13
*13:00 - 13 October, 2187 (Starship Krashaon, Michael 6 Quadrant)*


Mikita watched Zanthu as he tried to remember how to start up the Yagar-34.

"I thought you said you'd flown this before?" she said, impatiently.

"I have... well, my father let me hold the wheel when we were up in the air, but how difficult can it be?"

Zanthu pressed various buttons and pulled on random switches, but to no avail.

"Is it voice activated?" asked Mikita.

"I don't know!" replied Zanthu, angrily. It was the first time he'd snapped at Mikita.

"No need to shout, Zanthu," said Mikita.

"Yes, I know. I'm sorry, Mikita. Please, I just need a second to think..."

Zanthu closed his eyes and tried to remember what his father used to do on take-off. He always watched Qaanhu X when he was flying, looking over his shoulder, enthralled at the wonder of it all. There was a sequence of commands that needed to be carried out in a specific order. If he could only replay the images lodged somewhere in his mind.

"Let's see… Flight start lever: Up."

As he spoke he felt as if his father were there with him, guiding him through the procedures. His hands made their way to each of the controls and moved them assuredly into position.

"Ignition Temp 0.26 to standby… Check fuel load… Affirmative… Thrusters to manual… Nex-plates recharge set to 55… Flaps to detent…"

Zanthu smiled. "I think that's it, Mikita. We're ready to go."

Zanthu made a sign through the cockpit window to Leylaan, who was in the control booth to the left of the small craft. Leylaan gave a thumbs up and replied on radio: "Good luck, you two. Happy landings, when they come."

"Thanks Leylaan, I owe you," replied Zanthu.

"Yes, you do," said his brother. "Doors opening. You won't have long, brother. This will be reading up on flight deck. They'll be down in under a minute. Get going!"

"Roger, that."

Zanthu looked at the control buttons. Which one would take the craft forward and out of the docking area?

*Red? Green? It must be green. Green for 'Go', right?*

Zanthu held the controls in both hands and pressed the green button with his thumb. The Yagar-34 moved forward about 2 metres, then stopped.

"Shizzing Herra!"

Leylaan's voice came over the headset. "The red button, Zanthu. Green is for boosts."

Zanthu wasted no time. "Thanks again, big brother.

Zanthu pressed red and the Yagar shot out of the docking area.

As they left, Mikita saw Code guards bursting into the control booth and grabbing Leylaan. Their voices were loud in her earpiece, then - silence.

"They've got Leylaan, Zanthu!"

"He'll be OK, Mikita. They won't harm him."

"You seem pretty confident about that?"

"I am. He's my brother. Qaanhu X's first born. They won't hurt him. Punish him, maybe - but hurt him? No."

"And that doesn't bother you? The fact he will be

punished?"

Zanthu turned to look at Mikita. She was *frowning* at him. This was new, he thought.

"Yes, of course it bothers me. But I have to see beyond that, Mikita. I have to see the bigger picture."

"And running away is going to solve that, is it?"

"We're not running away, Mikita, we're *escaping*! Can't you see?"

Mikita shook her head in disagreement.

"So what, then? Would you rather stay here, alone, while I go to the priests for a year? Leave you here with my people? They'll treat you like a criminal, a freak! No. Once we figure out what to do, we'll come back. I'll think of something."

Mikita said nothing.

The Yagar-34 was a brilliantly fast craft. It sped on through space like a little dart of light. For a good few minutes Zanthu thought they were going to make good their escape.

"We'll do it, Mikita. Trust me."

Mikita looked at the scanner in front of her. To the rear of their craft were five dots, approaching rapidly.

"Can this thing go any faster, Zanthu?"

"I'm at full throttle, why?"

"Because they're on to us," she replied.

Then, Zanthu saw the fuel reading. It was at zero. "Wait! The tank is empty! But I just checked that. Before we took off!"

"Are you sure, Zanthu?"

But all this was of no consequence, the Intercepts were coming up fast at their rear.

Then a voice came over the line: "We have a lock on your craft, Zanthu. Please let go of the controls. We'll take it from here."

They were close enough now that Mikita could see the dragonflies painted on the side of the fighters.

Zanthu hit the panel in disgust. "Drain it!"

He watched as the Codes took control. Some buttons flashed on the panel in front of them, the Yagar banked to the right. Their escape was over almost before it had begun.

"Perhaps it's for the best, Zanthu," said Mikita.

"Perhaps you *should* go to the priests."

"No! I will not go there, to those... idiots! And that's final!"

But Mikita had more to say. "I'm going home, Zanthu. Back to Tapi-36. It's where I belong."

Zanthu was stunned. "But Mikita, we can't just sit back and let this happen. I'm Zanthu X, I'm supposed to be the leader of the Codes. And you are to be my wife, my queen."

"No, Zanthu. It's wrong. It's all wrong. These are *your* people. Not mine. You are right - I will always be an outsider here."

"Has it come to this, Mikita?" said Zanthu.

"Yes, Zanthu, I think it has," replied Mikita.

They sat in silence as the Yagar was brought back to the larger loading bay of the Intercepts. Neither one could look at the other. Time, it seemed, had run its course on their relationship.

## Chapter 14
*13:23 - 13 October, 2187 (Grafuulen, Tapi-36)*

They cut a strange figure, the two of them, as they walked down Klingdorfer Stratis - Sempre in Ichiro's suit, Polo in Mayette's dress, the slight buzzing sound of the NITs under Sempre's hat. But no one paid much attention. They looked like a badly dressed father and daughter out for a stroll. Little did they know...

Sempre stopped and pointed to a sign above a store.

'Steve's Emporium of Games and Toys'.

"This it?" asked Polo.

Sempre nodded.

He'd been there before, as a child. His father had taken him on a rare 'father and son' outing. He didn't remember much about the place, except that he'd been left to play with an old Earth-based GI Joe doll while his father disappeared for an hour or so, emerging later with a patch over one eye. Sempre had thought it odd at the time, but Sashan did many odd things, and Sempre knew better than to ask why. He knew he'd be given short shrift, if not a hair-drying telling off for being so impertinent.

From the outside it was a speciality store that catered for old toys. It wasn't particularly popular with the

Grafuulen's as it was a dusty old place full of things like 4D screens, Z-Boxes, old board table games, foosball and pinball machines etc. Old-fashioned stuff that nobody but collectors were really interested in. Boffiny types with personal hygiene issues like Keith in Muhaze. But on the inside, out in the back, there was a highly spec'd augmentations facility. The best on Tapi-36. TAPCON sent their agents there that were working undercover, or on secret missions in other parts of the Quadrant. It had to be a covert set-up: Augs were banned by the IFS.

As Sempre pushed open the front door, a little bell rang, inciting an admiring 'Ahhhh' from Polo. And if you could imagine that the little bell had then knocked a small ball down a track that in turn set off a multitude of other domino-effect-gadget-sorta-thingys, all climaxing in a fried egg in a pan, then you would be imagining the place correctly.

From the back of the shop came a small man with one tuft of hair in the middle of his head and one over each ear. He had a small, white, goatee beard trimmed into the shape of a snake's tongue, and small pince-nez glasses. His clothes were in an Earth-based Alpine style. Such that he could burst into a plaintive song about goatherds and puppets at any moment.

An old 'flat-screen' TV was switched on behind the counter. The volume was down but Sempre shifted uneasily when he noticed they were replaying the footage from Paradi Square. He kept the brim of his hat down over his eyes.

"Good morning, sir… and ma'am. What can I do for you this fine day?" asked the man.

Sempre remembered there was a secret message for the Augs. He'd put it in place when he became President - changed the old one: "I wonder if you have the Hornby 00 Gauge 'Flying Scotsman'?

"Ah," began the little fellow, with a subtle air of recognition. "Would that be the Class A1or A3, sir?"

"Why, the A3, please," replied Sempre, giving the correct answer.

"And does the gentlemen require track?"

Sempre knew the reply. "No, but I need the Stationmaster to help with my baggage."

The man smiled. "You have been here before, I see, sir. Please, come this way."


Steve.

That was his name. He had no last name, just Steve. He was standing over his tools straightening them, checking them for damage and cleanliness when the little Alpine man buzzed on the intercom and opened the door through to the back.

Steve was a tall man. He was dressed in an immaculate white lab coat and had a spherical deflector headpiece in position on his forehead, rubber gloves on his hands and a pen in his chest pocket. In short, a stereotypical surgeon, though this one didn't play golf in the afternoons. Instead, he played foosball next door in the shop.

"Thank you, Herr Dave," said Steve, to the little man. His eyebrows arched when he saw the two figures in the doorway. "But wait, this does not look like my 2pm patients?"

"No, sir," replied Herr Dave. "They're not."

"Then why are they here?"

"This gentleman needs to see the 'Stationmaster', sir." Dave winked when he said the latter.

"Ah, an railways *aficionado*. Why didn't you say so."

"I did, sir. Just then."

"So you did." Steve turned to Sempre. "Well, what can I do for you, sir? Or is it your daughter that needs some assistance?"

Sempre took off his hat, revealing his face.

Steve, if he had been a bird, would have fallen off his perch. "By Herra's jodhpurs! Mr. Sempre, sir!" he blootered. "But you're dead! I mean, obviously you're not dead, because, well, here you are! Oh, excuse my manners! I'm honoured, and shocked!"

Gradually, Steve got a grip.

"But what can I do for you, sir? Please, anything you wish. Your father was a great man, sir. And a wonderful Patron of the Augs."

Without a word, Sempre began to take his suit off.

With each piece of clothing he removed, so each muscle of Steve and Dave's face tightened and seemed to wince out loud. Soon Sempre was down to his shorts and his mother's body was exposed in all of its hideous glory.

"I want you to fix this," he said.

Steve gulped. "Um... right," he mumbled, assessing the task before him. "Fix, you say... In what *way*, sir?"

"I want you to reunite my head with my body."

Steve looked confused. He could see that Sempre's body was not his own. "But where are the parts, sir? Where is your body."

"It's frozen, in cryo. In Muhaze."

"Very good, sir. But I'm only a humble Augs man. I'm not an expert in the Cryro field, so to speak. It's a bit too, how shall I put it... *subtle* for my skill-set. I mean, I can whack in a snake-shaped diodometer for you, or install an extra pair of eyes for you, sir. And the new moving tattoos, no problem. That's all very rudimentary. But a head to a body. This is not the place for -"

Suddenly, Sempre roared. The little tufts of hair on top of Herr Dave's ears almost got blown off, it was so violent.

"Then where can I go!?" demanded Sempre. "Tell me!" The NITs buzzed strongly around the brim of his hat on the floor.

Steve clocked the electric bugs and became (quite rightly) highly nervous.

"Dr. Tamashito is your man, sir. But he's on the good-guy's side now, as you will no doubt know."

"Yes, I know that, fool! I employed him! Who else is there?"

There was a short pause as Steve and Herr Dave looked towards the ceiling deep in thought - before Polo spoke.

"Quasar," she said, softly. "Quasar would know someone."

"Yes, he would," said Steve, obviously well aware of the name. "But you'd be mad to get involved with an individual like him. On any level."

Sempre ignored Steve's warning. "Where is this *Quasar* fellow, then?" he said, looking at first Steve and then at Polo.

Steve shrugged his shoulders.

"I know where to find him," said Polo.

# Chapter 15

"The airfield, Jameson. That's where the power station is going to go," explained Spalding. "It's going to be a big mother. The biggest ever seen on any planet. Now look, you know the locals, the 'good' people of Tapi-36. I want you to smooth things over with President Swish and her cronies. Smile, be nice. Tell everybody how this is going to make Tapi-36 the most important planet in all the galaxies. You concentrate on that, I'll run things up front."

Jameson nodded hesitantly. "And what's the source of power for this set-up?"

Spalding deflected. "I'm sorry I can't tell you that. At least, not just now."

"Why? I think I should know what I'm getting myself into."

"Jameson, you're 'getting yourself into' a very important and highly confidential job given you by your *employers*. Oh, by the way, do you know where Jon-7 is? I heard he was locked up somewhere."

"Yeah, he's locked up. President Swish has him in the Muhaze Pen. Why? What good is he to us?"

"Oh, it's always handy to have somebody to take the rap - should anything go wrong. There is a problem though... On Tapi-36. It appears that David Sempre has mysteriously reincarnated"

"I'm sorry, Spalding. I don't follow you."

"Always slow on the uptake, weren't you, Jameson. David Sempre has risen from the dead. He's had some kind of resurrection. He's now got a hostage and wants his Presidency back."

"But how can that be? He was killed in the Froome Skirmish."

"It appears the Specialists are to blame. Somehow they got hold of his body and, in some kind of sick joke, attached it to his mother's."

Jameson looked amazed. "You're joking, right?"

"Oh, this is no joke, Captain. Quite the contrary. He is a dangerous man. And as the saying goes: 'Hell hath no fury like a woman scorned'. Best keep an eye on this, Jameson. We don't want any trouble. Oh, and I've made arrangements for you to go to Tapi-36 immediately."

"But the presentation? I'm needed here. I'm the Captain of this starship."

"Not necessary, Jameson. McGilvary will cover for you. It's already been arranged," replied Spalding, already leaving the Stateroom.

Jameson buzzed the Comms device. "Lead-Out, get me information on this Sempre business on Tapi-36. And find out why wasn't I informed?"

"Yes, sir. Right away."


Alone in the Stateroom, Jameson felt a 'Captain's instinct' moment similar to the feeling he'd got on Baal-500. He was right then, TAPCON had conned him. He had the same feeling now, except this time it was the IFS that was making him twitch.

*

"Maybe there is something we can do at the Crossing Point, when we all engage together. Is there a point where any of you see the source, or feel that you are close to the source?" Linden asked.

The remaining six Peers were brainstorming ideas to rid themselves of their powers. Cy had decided that because everybody felt so strongly about the GC, he would trust their judgement.

"I know that when we are in Sanctuary - that's when I feel closest to the source," said Ellery.

"Me too," added Cy.

"And me," joined Newton.

"Well, we should investigate that as soon as possible, said Linden.

"But when?" asked Marcie. "The docking is in an hour. Then the photo call, then off to Herra knows where."

"Yeah, and who's to say that we'll all be together after that?" said Tora. "They might split us up?"

That thought hadn't crossed their minds.

"Well, in that case," began Linden. "We have an hour."

*

Gompi and Charly got on the Number 5 street-tram heading north, through town, then on to the Uni buildings.

The streets were back to normal. Muhazians were going about their business as if the morning's trouble had not even happened. They all seemed so carefree. But that feeling did not adhere to the two mutants. They sat on the bus as two worried individuals, concerned for the future of their home planet.

"So many people," said Charly.

"Yes," replied Gompi. "So many…"

"I hope they nice to little Gompi."

"Me too," replied Gompi, then looked across at his girlfriend. "I sure they will be, Charly. I sure."

*

"I see the Crossing Point!" exclaimed Marcie. "Is everybody here?" She looked around, counting. "Four, five and Tora, six. Good that's everyone."

"Linden, what do we do now?" asked Cy.

76

"Well, let's find the direction we feel is closest to the source. Enter into Sanctuary, Peers."

They did so, and soon they saw before them the pulsing yellow core that let them know they were in the zone.

"How do people feel about this?" asked Linden.

"Not strong enough," said Newton.

"What about getting closer?" asked Ellery.

The Peers followed Ellery's lead and made their way through Sanctuary. They had never been told to go beyond that point. They were in unknown territory.

"I'm scared, Marcie," said Cy.

"It's OK, we're all together, Cy. We'll be alright."

From behind Sanctuary came a sensation of power and knowledge that struck the Peers as being the origins of the Golden Circuit. A small pinpoint of light was radiating the most ferocious beam of yellow that seemed like it was pushing them away.

"This must be it!" said Newton.

"Now, Peers," began Linden. "We don't know what effect this will have, but try and remove yourself from its hold. It's strong. So strong. Can you feel it? Imagine that you are taking off your skin. Like a snake. It is the only way I can think of doing this!"

Each of the Peers wrestled with Linden's metaphor, guiding their minds through a disrobing of their essential GC being. Letting it free itself from the grasp of the all-consuming ochre power.

Suddenly, the ground underneath them began to shake and tremor. The Golden Circuit was moving against them, sensing their mutiny.

The rumbling got worse. Cy fell over.

"Disengage, Peers!" shouted Linden. "Disengage!"

There was a flash of white light, then - darkness.

## Chapter 16
*13:55 - 13 October, 2187 (Grafuulen, Tapi-36)*

"This is the place," said Polo, then shook her head. "I can't believe I'm taking you here."

"Sounds like you have happy memories of your visits to this noble establishment," said Sempre, unimpressed.

The door to Quasar's backstreet joint opened suddenly. Frank came out, but the sight of Polo stopped him in his tracks.

"You!" he said, surprised and annoyed in the same breath. "What the shizz are you doing here? I thought I told you not to come back?" Then, he saw Sempre. "And with your old man, too! I tell you, you've got some nerve."

Lil' Jimi, Quasar's bodyguard and doorman, appeared behind Frank. "You got a problem there, Frank?"

Frank nodded towards Polo. "Yeah. Look what the fuurkat brought in."

"Oh," said Lil' Jimi. "It's him again, huh?"

Then Sempre lifted his brim and gave the two chiselers a crooked smile - it was the only one he had. The two thugs recognised him instantly.

"What the...?" they said, together.

Sempre look pleased with himself. "Ah, I see you

78

gentlemen know who I am. Good. Now, if you'll kindly introduce me to your 'Mr. Quasar', then we can all get on with our day."

They both stepped out of Sempre's way.

Frank, gestured inside. "This way, Mr. Sempre, please," he said, as Lil' Jimi reached for the door.

During his time in charge of Tapi-36, Sempre had always been good to the drug lords and the illegal goods criminals. Blackmail and embezzlement worked wonders in the hands of a master manipulator like David Sempre, and whatever he'd done for the underworld during his reign still seemed to hold currency now. It was all part of being a politician.

In his office, Quasar was in his usual position, behind his desk, twirling his blade, as Frank knocked on his door.

"Yeah, what is it?" came the jaded reply from inside.

"Um, sir, you got visitors. Someone you'll defo want to see, sir."

There was a pause inside, then Quasar said: "Ok, bring 'em in."

Frank opened the door.

Quasar's eyes bulged - and it wasn't the cocktail of banned substances in his bloodstream that had caused this reaction. "Holy Herra-ing shizz on a stick!" he said, getting up out of his seat.

Sempre brushed off the outburst. "Mr. Quasar," he began, matter of factly. "Now listen closely, I want you to help me. Can you give me the name of a good surgeon who can reattach my head to my original body? Know of anyone? Just off the top of your head? So to speak."

Quasar's jaw was still on the floor. He shook his already frazzled lid. "Lil' Jimi, tell me I'm not dreaming?"

"No, Quasar, this ain't no dream, sir. This is as real as my wife's charge account."

Sempre gave Quasar a look of mock concern. "You seem perturbed by our company, Mr. Quasar," he said, his brow furrowing.

"Yeah... I mean... No, Mr. Sempre. It's just... Hey, aren't you supposed to be dead?"

"Hmmmm, everyone seems to being asking me that question today. But, clearly, no, I'm not dead. I'm standing in front of you as your rightful President. Alive and well. But forget about that... Look, I can assure you that you'll be generously rewarded for your troubles, once I have been returned to my former glory. Rest easy that you will be able to retire a happy, if slightly odd, man."

Quasar's head was nodding. "Yeah, yeah. OK. Let me think... Right, you should go to see Ramrod. You got transport?"

"We did. But I'm afraid we've - how shall I put it - parked it in a tight spot. Perhaps you have a vehicle for hire?"

"Yeah, sure, Mr. Sempre. No problem. But why're you with him?"

"Him?"

"Yeah, Troy, there," he nodded towards Polo. "And why's he got a dress on?"

"Ah, I see what you mean. Well, 'Troy' and I are old friends. I knew his sister very well. But that is in the past. Do you have a problem with men in women's clothes?"

"Nah, Mr. Sempre. Not me. Whatever gets you through the night, that's what I say." Quasar looked at Polo suspiciously. "Frank?"

"Yes, boss?"

"Show Mr. Sempre and Troy here, how to get to Ramrod's, would you?"

"Sure thing, boss."

Quasar flinched. "Hey, what's that buzzing sound?"

"Ah, that is the sound of my little friends here." Sempre took off his hat to reveal the NITs.

Quasar got up from his seat. "Hey! What're they? What's going on here? Is this some kind of set-up?"

"No, no, Mr. Quasar," replied Sempre. "Nothing of the sort."

Quasar was still in a paranoid panic. "Frank. Lil' Jimi, go check the front. I'm not taking any chances, this is just too weird."

Quasar was Earth-based freaking out. Obviously a few too many loob-joobs in his coffee that morning.

"Hey, Quasar," said Polo, "take it easy, we're only

here for the info then we're gone."

Suddenly the sound of sirens could be heard in the distance.

"Holy shizzing mother of Herra!" shouted Quasar, reaching into his desk.

Sempre watched the degenerate closely. "NITs?" he said, warily. "Sempre says..." He paused as he waited to see what Quasar was going to do next.

Quasar took out a blaster. And aimed it at the two of them.

"'Kill Quasar!'"

The drug lord had no chance. The NITs were on him instantly.

After a few seconds of NIT feasting, he slumped to the floor, his brains spilling out through his nostrils.

Polo looked away. "Oh, shizz. That's disgusting!"

The NITs returned to Sempre, their bloodlust sated.

Sempre smiled at his power. His time on ice had clearly made no difference to his brains molecular structure - he was still emotionally derelict - despite the maternal influence of his mother's body

"A bit too much for your stomach, Miss Smith?" he said.

Polo gave him a look, as Frank and Lil' Jimi rushed back through the door. "Quasar," began Frank, "looks like the cops are..." - he stopped when he saw his boss' body on the floor. "Hey, what's going on? What've you done to Quasar?"

"The same thing that's going to happen to both of you if you don't do as I say," said Sempre, casually.

Frank saw the NITs buzzing around Sempre. "OK, OK, cool it, Mr. Sempre. Everything's hunky-dory. We're with you now. I never liked the man, anyways," he said, turning his gaze from Quasar's body. "Just keep those bugs away from me, alright?"

Sempre paused, then spoke: "NITs? Sempre says: 'Under my hat'." The NITs returned beneath his brim.

There was a loud knock at the front door, followed by a shout: "Open up!"

"Follow me," said Lil' Jimi, gesturing out the back. "I'll take you to see Ramrod."

## Chapter 17
*14:03 - 13 October, 2187 (Grafuulen, Tapi-36)*


Kané knocked again. Louder this time. He was beginning to get worried. Those sirens were getting awfully close. The withdrawal was tugging at him again, he was beginning to feel the pangs. He didn't like that feeling. He knew what would happen next. He needed to get inside.

"Hey, Frank! Jimi! Open up it's me, Kané!"

There was no answer.

"Frank, where the shizz are you?!"

He turned and looked down the street. No police cars, but the sirens were much louder now.

"Hey, Lil' Jimi! You taking a nap?"

No reply.

Kané took a few steps back and ran at the door with his shoulder. He hit it with good force but all it did was give him an ache that would later turn into a nasty bruise.

He tried again.

Nothing.

The door was thick and heavy. There was no way he'd get this to open up.

"Drain it!"

He rattled the door knob in disgust and turned away,

his mind beginning to race with panic. He needed those drugs - and fast.

A police car flashed past the alleyway.

"Oh, almighty shizz!"

Kané looked left and right for an escape route. The alley was a one way street. There were no fire escapes to climb up and away to the rooftops. He turned again to look at Quasar's door - and did a double-take as he noticed it was slowly opening.

"How the draining…?" Then it dawned on him that it hadn't been locked in the first place. "Oh, man!"

Kané didn't waste anymore time, he was inside the drug den and searching for Quasar's stash.

As he checked the various rooms in Quasar's lair he wondered where everyone was. It was very unusual for there to be nobody here. Quasar kept his stuff well-guarded at all times.

Eventually, he found some Nans that had been left out on a table. A good supply that would last him several weeks.

*This is really weird,* he thought to himself.

He could hear cars pulling up outside.

Kané realised he'd made a mistake. He should have left when he'd had the chance.

He made his way to Quasar's office to head out the back door.

Voices were coming from the alley.

As Kané entered the office he saw the drug lord's body on the floor.

Kané knew he was in trouble.

He turned around and saw five policemen pointing their guns at him.

"Don't move!" said one of the men.

"I've no intention of doing anything," replied Kané. "Look, there's been a mistake. It's not what you think. I just came here to -"

"Shut it, sonny!" said the police officer. "Put your hands in the air. Slowly! Keep them out front where we can see them."

Kané did as he was told. The cop motioned to one of the men, who promptly came over to Kané, brought his arms down roughly and handcuffed him.

"Clementi, get the forensic team over here, pronto. And Benson, seal the area. OK, Pritchard, get this slimeball back to Muhaze and radio in that we have a suspect in the Sempre case."

"Sempre case?" exclaimed Kané. "Are you mad? I've got nothing to do with -"

The policeman suddenly swung at Kané, catching him full on the jaw and sending him to his knees in pain.

"Look, boy. I'm not having a good day. Anymore backchat comes to mind, keep it to yourself, d'ya hear me?"

Kané felt blood in his mouth. He spat it to the floor.

"Do you hear me?!" the officer shouted.

Kané looked up at the officer. "Yeah. I hear you," he said.

The officer turned to his man. "Pritchard, take him away."

Pritchard shoved Kané down the hallway and out into the alley. It was filled with police cars, their flashing blue lights swirled around the street lighting it up like an aquarium. A gaggle of people had stopped to watch at the end of the lane, necks craning around the bits of street furniture in an attempt to get a glimpse of the events. Pritchard opened the door of the last police car and placed his hand on Kané's head as he pushed him down and into the vehicle. Kané fell forwards awkwardly and ended up in a faceplant on the backseat. He wriggled himself upright and watched Pritchard as he motioned for the two cops in the front to roll down their window so he could talk to them. Pritchard's tone had its customary self-important lilt: "Take him in, boys. Captain Hughes will be downtown in five. Clean him up and get him into the Q&A room, a.s.a.p."

"Roger, Pritch."

"And don't rough him up too much, leave that for Hughes," Pritchard grinned.

"Sure thing, Pritch. Just polish up the knuckledusters for the boss, huh?"

"You got it, Riddley."

The car reversed out of the alley, scrambling the rubberneckers in all directions. Riddley put his foot down and his partner switched on the siren.

They sped off down the street like they were heading for a pancake and bacon breakfast at Gretchi's - coffee refills at no extra charge.

Kané shook his head. What else could go wrong in his life right now?

Little did he know...

*

In their Holdings Quarters, the Peers began to come to, one by one.

"Ugh, my head," said Marcie. "It feels like I've been stood on by Earth-based elephants."

Tora sat up. "Me too."

The other Peers followed the two girls, each one feeling the after-effects of their disengagement.

"Disengaging always hurts, doesn't it?" said Newton. "Why is that?"

"Guru Teluthaan used to say that it was like unplugging something from the wall, rather than switching it off at the source," replied Cy. "The power seems to override itself, or something. I can't remember what exactly."

Linden spoke: "But listen, we found out something, didn't we?"

"What, Linden?" asked Tora. "That we failed?"

"On the contrary, Tora."

"How's that?"

"The GC. It was scared. It knew what we were up to, and it got frightened. How else do you explain the tremors?"

"Linden's right," said Ellery. "I could feel fear in there, and it wasn't coming from us."

"Exactly," said Linden. "So, we must try again. We must force the GC to hear us. To recognise our actions. C'mon we must try again. Is everyone OK?"

The Peers nodded groggily, no one seemed to be unduly affected.

Suddenly, Marcie's Comms device buzzed.

## Chapter 18

*14:04 - 13 October, 2187 (Sellicha Starship, Michael 6 Quadrant)*

A tear fell from Mikita's eye as she watched the Krashaon disappear into the distance. *Another relationship chalked up to experience,* she thought, as she turned away from the window and sat down on her bed in her quarters. She was in pain, like no other heartbreak she'd experienced, and deep down she was disappointed in herself. She hadn't ready for this. She wasn't ready to be a a married person, let alone a queen. She thought that it was the right thing, that this was what she wanted, but she'd been wrong. She loved Zanthu, but everything was happening too quickly. Maybe, at some point in the future, they might find each other again, but for now…

Her door buzzer chirruped.

Mikita got up to answer it.

Standing there was Garthh. One of the lower ranked officers, and one of only five Codes sent with Mikita to escort her back to Tapi-36. He was in his mid-20s, blonde, as all Codes were, with grey eyes speckled with orange. He smiled when she answered.

"Oh, hello, Garthh," said Mikita, wiping her tears away. "Can I help you?"

"Good afternoon, Miss Smith. I have come to -" He paused for a second -he'd noticed her wiping her face. "I'm sorry. Shall I come back later?"

Mikita shook her head. "No, no. Please, go on. Do you have a message for me or something?"

"Um, yes. I was to tell you that we will arrive in Muhaze in 6 hours, ma'am."

"6 hours? That's quick."

"Yes. The Sellihca is a speedy craft. She is small, but fast as light. Well, not quite that fast." He smiled.

Mikita was grateful for some light conversation, after all she had been through. "Good. That's good, Garthh. I am keen to get home quickly. Thank you for letting me know."

"It is my pleasure, Miss Smith. Now, may I bring you something to eat or drink? We can make anything you wish."

Mikita was about to say no, out of politeness, then realised she was starving - some comfort food was in order. "Yes, you can, Garthh. I would like some Earth-based tomato soup. Can you do that?"

"Of course, ma'am. I will program the Food Designer and I shall bring you that in a little while. Is there anything else I can do for you?"

"No, that will do fine, Garthh. Thank you."

Garthh nodded and turned to go.

"Oh, Garthh?"

"Yes, ma'am?"

"Was there anything from Zanthu? Any message at all?"

The Code shook his head. "No, ma'am. I'm sorry. There is no message."

Mikita half-smiled. "OK. Thank you, Garthh."

The Code nodded, and left for the kitchens.

Mikita went back into her room and opened her suitcase to find fresh clothes when she saw something. Something she'd packed but had completely forgotten about. In the side pocket of the inside of the case she'd placed the Comms device she'd got from Marcie in there before she'd left. She'd forgotten about with all the furore. She took it out now and looked at it. It was beautifully made. Mikita thought about her friends from

Plaateux-5. They would be on their way to the reunion with their families by now - onboard the Argon with her father, Captain Jameson. *Lucky them*, she thought. She would give anything to be with them now. She truly missed them.

But self-pity was no longer going to feature in Mikita's life. She'd decided to give that a wide berth from here on in. *You make your own destiny*, she told herself. And with that thought she flicked on the Comms device. The little machine had a dial on the top that flashed green and whizzed round this way and that. It looked like it was trying to pick up a signal. Marcie had said it was powerful, and the read-out below listed hundreds of available intercepts. Mikita scrolled through them but didn't see anything that particularly caught her eye. Then she saw one that read 'Peer001Mar'.

"Ha!" she exclaimed.

Underneath that was 'Peer002Ell', then 'Peer003New' and so on, up to 'Peer007Lin'. The last three letters of the intercept were the first three initials of each of the Peers names: Mar = Marcie, Ell=Ellery, New=Newton, and so forth. Mikita scrolled back to Marcie and pressed a small, blue button that said 'connect'. The Comms device made a distorted hum, then blinked twice and pronounced: "Connection affirmative. Please speak now."

Mikita didn't know what to say. "Um, hello? Marcie? Are you there?"

Marcie's voice crackled back: "Mikita? Mikita is that you?"

Mikita squealed with excitement. "Yes, Marcie! It's me! How are you? Where are you?"

"We're onboard the Argon." Mikita heard muffled voices off. It sounded like Marcie was telling the Peers that Mikita was on the line. "Sorry, we're on our way to meet our parents. We're all a bit over-excited. Where are you?"

"I'm going home. To Tapi-36."

"Oh, I thought you were with Zanthu on the Krashaon?"

"I was but things haven't worked out. I'm going home."

"Oh that's a shame."

"Yeah, well. Shizz happens."

"Indeed it does," replied Marcie. "Hey, do you want to talk to everyone? I'll put you on speaker phone?"

"Yes! Please. Do it, Marcie!"

Mikita heard a change in the reception as Marcie set her Comms device to 'Room'.

"Um… hello, everybody!"

Mikita heard the group reply 'Hello, Mikita!'

Marcie came on again. "Hey, listen, Mikita. Something's come up here."

"Oh, yeah? Sounds ominous."

"It is. But we're working on it. Mikita, we've decided to give up our powers to the -"

But then the line went dead.

Mikita was left dumbfounded. *Give up their powers to… What?*

# Chapter 19
*14:05 - 13 October, 2187 (Muhaze, Tapi-36)*


Gompi and Charly were waiting in the foyer of the Mu-U as Dr. Tamashito approached them from the sliding doors of the lift.

"Ah, Gompi. Good to see you," said the doctor, extending his hand. "And this must be Charly. A pleasure to meet you."

Charly shook the Doctor's hand. "Thank you for seeing us, Dr. Tamashito. We know you busy man."

"Never too busy for an old friend like Gompi."

Dr. Tamashito gestured to the sofas near the large glass windows of the foyer. "Please, sit down. And tell me how I can help."

As they sat down, Charly began to explain. "Dr. Tamashito. We see you on news. You great expert. We need you help, please."

"Of course. Tell me how I can be of assistance?"

"We scared for world," said Gompi. "You see, we order a little Gompi, yesterday, from Repro-Life Clinic, and we worried about future for little one. This planet, it always have things go wrong. Bad people in charge, war, Froome, TAPCON. And now, Mr. Sempre, he back."

"Yes, Gompi," replied Dr. Tam. "But I think... well, I hope, Janeee Swish will be able to contain the problem. She is a very capable young woman."

"Oh yes," said Charly, "we like President Swish. We big fans."

Tamashito smiled. "Good. That's good, Charly. She's the right person in the right place, at the right time, I believe."

Gompi carried on, "Dr. Tamashito, we want ask you - can you send update to mutants? Like with Mikita Smith. Can you do this?"

"Well, Gompi. I'm working as a teacher now, ever since the last Froome Skirmish. The mutant upkeep is now in the hands of President Swish, and I'm not sure who is in charge of her Science Programme. You see, when the TAPCON Towers building was destroyed so was the central computer system. Bigsby, it was called. It sent the updates. Now, it's just junk in the Kasturba dump, along with all the other rubble from the TAPCON regime. Why? How can an update help?"

"We thought you send update to help catch Mr. Sempre," said Charly.

"Yes, save the planet," joined Gompi. "Make it nice for little Gompi, and all little people."

Tamashito smiled. "It is a noble idea. But, as I say, I think that Janeee Swish has things under control."

Gompi looked at Charly. He saw the disappointment in her eyes. "Yes, you right, Dr. Tam. You a wise man, Dr. Tam. We go home. We wait. President Swish, she will sort it out."

The two mutants got up, made a short bow to the Doctor, and left.

Tamashito watched them walk out the front doors of the Mu-U main building and down the steps towards the No. 5 street-tram stop. He felt bad that he couldn't, or rather, wouldn't help his old friend. But he was a full-time teacher now. He didn't want to get involved in anymore shenanigans with Sempre, or bring up the old memories of his past life with TAPCON. There was so much pain connected with those thoughts: his family held hostage for all those years; being blackmailed into doing dirty work for TAPCON. He'd had no choice in those dark times. Either comply with Sempre's wishes or his family would die. Doing a TV show with Phinn and Harriet Honeste was one thing, but getting involved? No. That wasn't for him, not anymore.

But still, Sempre's return *had* disturbed him. His analytical brain couldn't help but be intrigued by Sempre's physical appearance - he was half female/half male! How did it happen? What was going on? Tamashito was sure that this had been the work of the Specialists. But why would they do such a thing?

Tamashito remembered that the Specialists used a bunker somewhere out near the Airfield, a lab that Quince and Mitchell maintained for their more 'experimental' work. The airfield was being dug up at this very moment, but perhaps… just perhaps, it was worth a trip, to see what he could find? Information on the NITs, perhaps? Or Sempre's transformation? It wouldn't hurt matters to have a look, would it?

Tamashito decided to go out for half an hour, if nothing turned up he would come home and forget all about it. Besides, it was already afternoon and he would need to pick his children up from school at 4pm.

He went back upstairs to get his things and headed out to the Mu-U car park.

Ten minutes later he was at the old airfield.

It had changed, somewhat.

Ambulance warning lights filled the air with circular swirls of red, while Police cars sirens provided pockets of blue in the dusty atmosphere. There was a frantic rush to the proceedings that Tamashito hadn't seen since the Froome attack. It made him anxious.

*Just a half hour, then I'll go home…*

The bodies of the murdered workmen were being loaded up into the ambulances; but there were no survivors here. Sempre's NITs had done their job well.

Tamashito got out of this car and made his way over to one of the ambulances. A blood-stained medic recognised him.

"Dr. Tamashito. What brings you out here, sir? Not a pleasant picture, I'm afraid."

"Oh, it's work related, Doctor. I've come to find something. Do you mind if I look around?"

The medic was covering a dead workman's face with a sheet. "Help yourself, Dr. Tam. But there's not much here except... well, just be careful, sir."

Tamashito nodded. "Thank you. I will."

The Doctor watched as the stretcher bearers loaded the body into the ambulance. There were already two more sheet-covered bodies in the rear. He shook his head and walked away from the ambulance and on towards the airfield runways.

Tamashito wasn't exactly sure what he was looking for. Any entry to the bunker would be well hidden. Access to it would be known only to the Specialists - and perhaps to David Sempre, but that would be all. He needed to tap into the way their minds worked (if he could stand to do such a thing) to glean some sort of clue.

The Specialists shared a dark, scatological humour, he knew that much. Fiendishly intelligent, but with a love of the ridiculous and bizarre. Perhaps the entrance would be marked, if it was marked at all, with some sort of witty sign or slogan. Something out of the ordinary: 'Dead End' or 'Beware of the Dog'. Something that would make them laugh, but no one else.

Moving out past the medical vehicles Tamashito came to the beginning of the runway. At the sides of the long concrete strip was open scrubland. He began to search the undergrowth.

After fifteen minutes of spiky grass and burrs attaching themselves to his trousers he'd seen nothing out of the ordinary, no markings of a below ground access.

*What am I doing out here,* he said to himself. *Five more minutes and that's me done.*

Further on he saw a sign for North pointing the wrong way. The sign was buckled in the middle, and had obviously been damaged. Probably in the clean up process. As he walked on the scrub became thicker. He was about half way along the runway when he saw a wooden sign, hand painted. It read:

'Warning: Noise Sensitive Area'

Then below, in spray paint: 'Quiet! Great Minds At Work.

*This must be it.* thought Tamashito.

He began to search the immediate area around the sign

for an entry point, but found nothing of note.

Then he saw the hatch lid, cast aside by Sempre earlier that day. He noticed that the ground around it had been disturbed and showed footprints. The grass to the left of the hatch was worn down into a path - someone had been walking through there, headed toward the remains of the main buildings. Tamashito figured that was the route Sempre had taken before sending in his NITs.

Tamashito was certain this was the place.

He followed the bent over grass until he came to a hole. The hole had a metal ladder on the side, that disappeared down in the inky depths. He reached over and grabbed the top rung and was soon climbing down the ladder.

Tamashito wondered what he would find down there. He'd not brought any form of physical protection - a gun or blaster - should there be any trouble. He had a hand-held device, but that was it. Whatever was down there, he hoped it wasn't as vicious as Sempre's NITs.

After a good minute of climbing, Tamashito saw a tiny glimmer of light. It was dim but there was clearly some electricity still connected in the bunker. That was good news.

Finally, there was no more ladder to climb down. He was at the main passageway. He stepped off the ladder and looked left and right. The tunnel went both ways. Tamashito stroked his greying beard and decided to turn right, away from what he figured was a route back to the main buildings, where there would most likely be another entrance, perhaps for equipment deliveries to the mad doctors.

As he walked down the dark corridor, sparks flew off exposed wires and the hall lights flickered. He noticed more footprints in the dust that had settled. They looked like the ones from beside the hatch. Sempre had come from this direction, he was almost positive of that.

Up ahead, Tamashito saw the sliding doors of the Specialists lab. The retina scanner was shot to pieces, but the door was open.

He went in.

The main lab was strewn with debris. The blasting had caused the ceiling to become fragile and Tamashito sensed that he wouldn't have a lot of time to investigate the scene. He wandered through the large room, picking up bits of broken machinery, taking in what the two strange scientists had been up to.

Plans for the NITS were pinned out on the main table, casings for their bodies were arranged neatly on a metal tray, two large microscopes lined the counter to the right of the table, a whole array of tools and instruments all arranged neatly on the wall. However, everything was covered in dust from the blasts.

But there was more. Tamashito felt an unsettling atmosphere of death throughout the underground hideaway. He turned towards the rooms off the main lab and opened each door. In the first were the bodies of the rats used by Quince and Mitchell. The room was already reeking of the rotting rodents. He shut the door quickly and moved on to the second room. More equipment covered in dust. He recognised some of it, in fact, he'd signed off the contents of the boxes himself in days long past, and in the central area a plinth with apparatus for operations. Tamashito walked over to it and felt that it had been used, recently. Then, in the final room, he found the two corpses of Quince and Mitchell. Tamashito flinched at the sight of them, but went in to examine the bodies. Heavy bruising around both necks, dark red holes where their eyes once were. It was obvious they'd been choked to death. But it would have been something very powerful that had taken their lives, and it hadn't been the NITs. Tamashito didn't need all the brains he possessed to work out that that individual was one David Sempre.

Heading back into the lab, Tamashito found the Specialists main frame. It was still plugged into the wall but the power supply was fried. Tamashito taped up the cable, then replaced the fuse and plug and shoved it back into the socket. Pressing the start-up the hub sprung into life.

"That's more like it," said Dr. Tam.

Tamashito tapped away at the QWERTY until he found himself at the gateway to the old TAPCON network. The system looked garbled. There were bits of code missing all over the place. The Doc sighed as he began to piece together the programme he'd spent so long encoding years before. It was going to take him a while, and not a coffee pot in sight...

*

Holly Dreamo knew what had happened to her. She had been brainwashed by Aldoorin Anoote into believing that the complete destruction of mankind was the only possible solution to the problems of the Universe. She knew that she had been changed by the Guardians, forced to believe their philosophy by desperate means: the days spent in confinement, the drugs, the electro-shock treatment, it had broken her down, and quickly, too. But what defences did she have? She was only a little girl. Yet still she maintained the Guardians' beliefs. Despite the knowledge that she had been used by the Guardians; that she'd been turned into their pawn - despite *all* of this, she still believed their hideous message: 'Mankind was the curse of the cosmos and needed to be annihilated.'

Holly's cell was mid-ships, towards the rear of the Argon. Well away from the other Peers.

Her first instinct had been to escape. But the door was locked and bolted.

She'd tried accessing the Golden Circuit but for some reason it was ineffective. She didn't understand why.

She began to realise the only way out was through the door, and that meant manipulating her captors.

It was almost time for her appointment with Dr. Gössner. Each day at 10am, Dr. Gössner would appear at the door of her cell and knock. Today was no different. The knock sounded and Holly straightened herself out.

"Holly, it's Dr. Gössner."

"Hello, Doctor. Please come in." Holly was trying a new tack. She was pretending to be 'cured'. She was not going to protest wildly at everything that Dr. Gössner said, like usual. On the contrary, she would agree to it all.

Private Sawchuck let the doctor into Holly's cell. "Any problems, ma'am, I'm right here," he said.

"That's fine, Private. I shall call you if I need you."

Tina entered to a smiling Holly. She was sitting up straight on her bed ready for Dr. Gössner's first question.

Tina was immediately suspicious. "Good afternoon,

Holly. And how are you today."

"Good afternoon, Doctor. I'm wonderful today, thank you."

"Yes, I can see that."

"I'm feeling very happy and very positive. And I've been thinking about what you've been saying and I have come to the conclusion that you are right. The Guardians were wrong. Their ideas were wrong and everything about them was just plain wrong, wrong, wrong."

Tina's eyebrows raised. "Oh. Well that certainly is a turnaround. So you now believe that mankind does not need to be exterminated; that man is important to the universe?"

"Oh, yes. Very important."

"That's interesting."

"Yes, indeed it is... So, can you let me go now?"

"Well, I will need to report back to Captain Jameson, then he will need to inform the IFS, Mr. Reg Spalding in onboard now as its representative. But if you really feel that way, then this will benefit you when it comes to the trial."

Holly was suddenly agitated. "Trial!? I'm going on trial? For what?"

"Why, yes, Holly. You committed a crime on Plaateux-5. All those involved with the Guardians must stand trial. It is the law. But you are so young, you will not be sent to prison, more likely held at the juvenile detention unit on Mars."

"Mars?!" said Holly, horrified, her cover beginning to slip.

Tina recognised this, and carried on. "Yes, it's not so bad. You can have visitors, occasionally. Family, friends. I imagine most of them are on Earth, but surely they'd make the journey just for you?"

Holly looked like she would erupt, what with all the effort of keeping up her pretence.

Tina continued: "It wouldn't be long. A few years. Five, at most... perhaps."

"Five!"

"Yes, then you'd be out, free - if there was no appeal."

"Appeal?" She got up from her bed. Her mood had changed back to her normal aggressive demeanour.

"There's no way any of that's happening to me! Let me out of here!"

Holly ran to the door, then began banging her fists on it like an angry little chimp in an Earth-based zoo.

Private Sawchuck opened the door. He was holding a small stun gun. Holly tried to get past him but he caught her easily and held her so she couldn't move.

"Best use the gun, Sawchuck," said Tina, reluctantly.

Tina helped him restrain her as Sawchuck held the gun up to Holly's neck and pulled the trigger. A yellow-green light emerged from the barrel that knocked Holly unconscious. She slumped into Sawchuck's arms - he carried her over to her bed.

"That will be all, Dr. Gössner."

Tina turned. Reg Spalding was standing in the doorway.

"I will take things from here, doctor. Thank you."

"But, Mr. Spalding. We must check her vital signs after such a shock. It's ship protocol."

"I will do that. Now, please, leave me with the girl."

Tina looked at Spalding for a second before relenting. Spalding was high up the chain of command.

"Private Sawchuck, come with me," she said. "We will leave Miss Dreamo with Mr. Spalding."

"Yes, Dr. Gössner," replied the Private. He gently lay Holly out on her bed and followed Tina from the room.

Spalding's eyes watched them leave, then he turned to the young girl.

Spalding spoke out loud, like most psychopaths do, almost willing somebody to catch them; unafraid, so convinced are they by their own abilities.

"Now, Miss Dreamo, let's get you ready for action."

He took off his bag and opened the zip on the side, then pulled out a small device and brought it up to the back of Holly's head. With one swift movement he inserted a tiny chip into Holly's lower skull - she let out a soft groan as he did so, then fell back into her previous unconscious state.

"There. That didn't hurt too much now, did it?" said Spalding, smiling to himself. "That will tell me more about your friends' ideas of rebellion."

He packed up his things, then made his way back to his

quarters. The Turandot would be arriving shortly - he needed to make the necessary arrangements.

## Chapter 20
*14:06 - 13 October, 2187 (Muhaze, Tapi-36)*


As Lil' Jimi pulled away in Quasar's shabby wreck of a car, he did a U-Turn, allowing Polo to catch sight of the police arriving at the back alleyway. There were only two vehicles, but she knew that there would be more on the way, and soon the whole planet would be looking for her and Sempre - if they weren't already. She had wanted to escape from Sempre from the start, but she'd needed to be certain she would be able to get a clean getaway, after all Sempre had the NITs and he obviously wasn't afraid of using them. But now it was looking increasingly difficult for her to do so, any botched attempt and she would almost certainly wind up like Quasar.

"How far is it to this Ramrod's," asked Sempre.

"It's not far," said Lil Jimi. He then turned down a backstreet and parked the car.

"He was right," said Polo, with a grin.

"OK. Get out and follow me," said Jimi.

The big bodyguard led them to the end of the alley. Only a bare brick wall in front of them.

"What is this? Some kind of joke?" said Sempre, tetchily.

Lil' Jimi smiled at the old TAPCON boss and ran his

hand in front of a sign to his left that said 'Dead End Zone'. The brickwork directly below the sign fluttered like it was made of water, then settled back to its original state.

"Oh, very clever," said Sempre. "I wasn't aware that we had this kind of tech on Tapi-36. I would have used this myself had I known about it."

"There's a lot of things on this planet that you don't know about, Mr. Sempre," replied Frank.

"Yeah, OK, Frank. Save it for later," said Lil' Jimi. "Now, you guys go through. Frank you go first, show them how it's done."

"Sure thing, Jimi." Frank waved his hand over the sign and the brick did its magical dance. "Follow me," he said, as he walked straight through the wall.

Polo looked at Sempre. "Now I've seen everything," she said, in amazement.

"Come on, folks. I've not got all day," said Jimi, impatiently.

Sempre gestured for Polo to go ahead. "Ladies first, Miss Smith."

Polo stepped forward - and vanished.

"You next, Mr. Sempre," said Lil' Jimi.

Sempre looked warily at Lil' Jimi - then followed Polo through.


On the other side they found themselves in a small, high-ceilinged room with no windows, and walls made out of metal sheeting. A bare lightbulb swayed slowly from a beam. It was like a prison cell for insane, dangerous inmates.

Quite fitting, for Sempre, in truth.

A door at the far end opened and through it walked a skeletal man in a shiny grey suit, with white hair slicked backed neatly and tied in a pony-tail that was so short it seemed quite unnecessary. He wore spherical glasses with no rims and fine metal rods over the ears. On the left side of his head was an augmentation shaped like an Earth-based spider that covered his cheekbone, and whose legs that ran down over his temples, past a mean mouth to below his jawline. The Aug bleeped every few seconds, very quietly, and tiny blue lights ran the length of it as it did so. His eyes squinted continuously, as if he were suffering some great internal pain.

"Mr. Ramrod, I presume?" asked Sempre.

The man shook his head, then he opened his slit of a mouth to speak: "OK, Jimi, Frank - let's lock them down." His voice was coarse and high-pitched.

The two henchmen grabbed Polo and Sempre, holding them tightly while the strange man moved towards them. Polo struggled in an attempt to free herself, but Sempre didn't move a muscle.

"Don't you know who I am, sir?" he said.

The man just smiled a sick little smile. "Oh, we know who you are - son of Sashan - spawn of Froome."

From behind his back the man produced a small cylindrical device.

Sempre watched as the man brought it out in front of him, pressing the bottom of it with his thumb. A long needle rose up from the inside - a tiny drop of red liquid appearing at the tip.

He came close to Sempre, who still did not move and looked straight ahead. With one swift movement the white-haired man injected him in the neck with whatever horrible solution his vial contained. Sempre moaned and fell backwards into Lil' Jimi's arms.

He turned mechanically towards Polo. "Now, Miss Smith. Do not fret. It will not hurt you… much."

He pushed Polo's head to one side and thrust the needle into her neck.

Polo remained calm and did not struggle. She wasn't giving in to them - whoever they were

Everything went black as she slumped to the floor.

*

"It just cut off," said Marcie. "It doesn't usually do that. Not since the prototype. Then again, there was that time… Hmm… maybe I should have tested it more…"

"No, Marcie. It's perfect as it is. And besides, Mikita is a long way away," offered Tora.

"Yes, I suppose so," replied Marcie, glumly.

"Maybe she'll call again," said Cy.

Marcie nodded. "Yes, maybe. I'm sure you're right, Cy."

They waited for a few minutes, all of them staring at the device, but nothing happened. Mikita didn't called back.

There was a buzz at the Holdings door. It slid open revealing Reg Spalding.

"Ah, Peers," he began. "So good to see you all, again." His forced smile had 'supercilious' written all over it.

"The feeling's not mutual," whispered Marcie to Tora.

Spalding paused. He stared at Marcie. "Something you wish to share with us, Miss Llanethli?"

"No, Mr. Spalding. Nothing, sir," she replied.

Spalding took a step towards her. "But, what is that you have there?"

"Oh, it's nothing, Mr. Spalding. Nothing important."

"Let me see it, Marcie." He held out his hand and beckoned with his fingers. Marcie brought the device to him.

Spalding looked it over. "A Comms device. Homemade by the looks of it. Yes?"

"Yes, sir."

"Very well made. Almost professional."

Marcie smiled, despite herself.

"Can I borrow it, Miss. Llanethli? I would like to show this to someone."

Marcie had no option. "Yes, of course, Mr. Spalding."

Spalding went over to his briefcase and placed the device inside. He turned again to the Peers.

"Good. Now, as you will all be aware, the photo-call with your parents will take place shortly. I am here to instruct you on your conduct throughout the presentation. The press will be there and will be allowed questions. Your replies are crucial. You must answer *positively*. 'We are so proud to be a part of this venture', 'We are all looking forward to being ambassadors', this kind of thing. No negativity will be tolerated. Do you understand, children?"

*Children?* thought Linden.

*Children?* thought Tora.

*Children?* thought Cy.

"And what if we don't want to be ambassadors?" asked Ellery, his boldness getting the better of him.

Spalding walked slowly over to the young man from Seba-23. The leather heels of his shoes clipped away at the floor with an air of menace.

"Well, well, well. Do I detect dissention in the ranks?"

"What if there is?" said Ellery, taking a step forward. Ellery was being brave to the point of foolishness.

"Then you will have to pay the consequences, Mr. Greyslate."

"And they are...?"

"Do not push me boy," warned Spalding, his eyes narrowing. "You wouldn't like what happens next."

The door swished open and Dr. Gössner entered the Holdings rooms.

She stopped abruptly on noticing Spalding and Ellery's standoff. "Is there a problem here, Mr. Spalding? Ellery what is going on?"

Spalding was suddenly all oil and charm. "No, Dr. Gössner. Mr. Greyslate and I were just getting familiarised. Everything is completely fine. All is in order."

"Excellent," said Tina, giving Ellery a look. "Now Peers, I hope you have listened closely to what Mr. Spalding has said. It's very important that a good first impression is made. This is going out to thousands of planets all around the cosmos, and you don't need me to tell that that is a lot of people."

The Peers nodded.

Lead-Out arrived at the door: "They are ready for you now - Peers - Mr. Spalding. I gather the Turandot has now docked, so Peers, you can see the craft from the Stateroom. It is quite a sight."

# PART TWO

# 'Revenge'

## Chapter 21
*14:27 - 13 October, 2187 (Muhaze, Tapi-36)*


"C'mon, Kendall. Let's me and you take a trip downtown and live it up a little? What do you say, bro'?"

Kendall Crisp laughed. "Mr. 7, may I remind you that you are a prisoner? A man convicted of treason, embezzlement, the manufacturing of illegal currency, and countless other crimes that -"

"OK, OK, Crispy boy. No need to rub it in." Jon-7 looked uncharacteristically forlorn.

Kendall saw his demeanour and added: "But under any other circumstance, yes, it would be a joy, I am sure."

Jon-7 managed a grim smile. He had been in Muhaze Penitentiary for six weeks now, and was starting to feel the strain. For a start, he was unrecognisable - even to himself. His blonde locks had been shorn to a crew cut. His glamorous wardrobe replaced by a gym locker containing a single change of prison clothes, the Earth-based orange, jump-suit type, and a few pairs of pants and socks. On top of that, his domestic surroundings were not at all what he was used to. A toilet was, mercifully, en-suite, but consisted of a simple hole in the ground and a small hand basin. Showers were communal. Food served in the airless canteen. It was a lifestyle Jon-7 was alien to and it had dented his ego. Admittedly, this was something that needed a junkyard-like demolishing to bring it down to a normal person's level, but still, Jon-7 was taking it hard.

He'd even begun the early stages of self-questioning. He found himself waking at 4am, and instead of asking himself things like - 'What will I wear today?' or 'How shall I style my hair?' he was asking - 'Was I right to be so horrible to Budgie all the time?' or 'Was it OK to rig the election?' As of yet, he hadn't been able to answer any of those questions, but it showed a vast improvement in his inner person. Maybe it was something in the penitentiary's water? Maybe a bit of jail time was just what he needed?

"OK, Mr. Crisp, Mr. 7, we're ready for you now, sirs," called a crew runner.

Jon-7 turned to Kendall Crisp. "Listen, Kendall, do me favour and call me Jonathan when we're on screen? You see, that's my real name. I only put the number on the end to make it sound more flash. My real name is Jonathan Potts. Did you know that? Plain old Jonny Potts. That's really who I am. And from now on that's who I'd like to be known as. My days of swagger and bravado are gone. Tell Tapi-36 that. For me, would you? Let them know that Jon-7 is no more. Jonathan Potts is here to stay. Will you do that for me, Crisp, me old sausage?"

Kendall nodded. "Of course, Mr. 7... I mean. Mr. Potts. Um, Jonathan... It will be a pleasure."

"Mr. Crisp, you are on in 10, sir," said the runner.

The camera crew had started the countdown.

Kendall straightened his tie, smelt his breath on his hand and brushed imaginary specks off his jacket.

"5-4-3-2-1 - On air!"

Kendall beamed a glorious smile to his viewers.

His new daytime chat show 'Late Lunch With Kendall Crisp' was a success all over Tapi-36. He'd finally found his niche. A show with news, celebrity interviews and cookery tips. Kendall's mother was the former TV chef Fanny Crisp, now retired, but she'd taught her son how to bake and cook from an early age. Kendall was better than most of the chefs in Muhaze's top restaurants. It was the most popular part of his show. So much so, he had put out a book to go with the series: 'Nice 'N' Crisp: How To Fry

The Kendall Way.' Wok recipes, deep-fat fryer ideas and 101 uses for simple frying pan. It went straight into the bestseller list at number one. Yes, life was good for the new Kendall Crisp.

"Helooooo, Tapi-36. And welcome to another edition of 'Late Lunch With Kendall Crisp'. I'm here at the Muhaze Penitentiary where today I'm talking to a man who is one of the most infamous criminals in recent memory. Today, I'm with a certain Jon-7, or rather, Mr. Jonathan Potts. That's right viewers, you heard me correctly: *Jonathan Potts* is here with me. That is Jon-7's real name, by the way, and the name he has just informed me that he would like to be known by in the future." Kendall turned to Jon-7. "Isn't that right Mr. Potts?"

Jonathan came on screen. "Yes, that is correct, Kendall. Jon-7 is gone for good." To the audience he was hardly recognisable as his former spectacular self. Kendall knew this would be the case.

"And it would appear that life in jail is somewhat different to life in the outside world, would I be correct in saying that, Jonathan?"

"Oh, yes, indeed, Kendall. And I'm sure the viewers at home can see that I am a changed man in more ways than one." Jonathan laughed, and rubbed his hand through his buzz cut.

"Looking a little less shaggy there, Jonathan, that's for sure. But tell me, what is life like for you now? How are you being treated here in jail?"

"Oh, terrific. What a place! Great food. Great company. Couldn't be better. But it's not all lifting weights and playing ping-pong, let me tell you. No, I've been doing some real soul searching, doing some reading - and not just your new cook book, Kendall - ha! - no, I've been delving into Herra's great work and looking deep inside my soul. And do you know what I saw when I looked into those murky depths, Kendall?"

"No, Jonathan, tell us? What did you see?"

"I saw a man who had been a fool. I saw a man who'd been lost. I saw a man who needed to be saved. From himself. From his own misguided ways. And that man, Kendall, was me. Or rather, the old me. The 'Jon-7' me. Oh yes, that man was a reprobate, a loser, a heinous doer of wrongs. But he's gone now. Cast out, never to return again…"

"Hmmm. Powerful words there, Jonathan," Kendall said, sagely. "But tell us more. Tell us about your road to salvation."

Jonathan looked down at the floor, acknowledging the difficulty of his task. "When I think back to the things I did, I feel a profound shame. I feel a gut-wrenching torment that I can't go back in time and right those wrongs. I would happily spend the rest of my life doing just that, if it were possible. But there are no time-machines, are there Kendall? There is no way back to the past. No way to fix my mistakes. All I can do is pray for forgiveness, and look forward to a time when I can be at peace with my soul. For sure, it's a long, long walk down that lonely path, but that is where I'm heading. I'm all packed up and ready to go. I'm putting on my rucksack of retribution. Herra, protect me - and everybody out there too, Kendall." Jonathan wiped a tear from his eye, and real or not, the viewers at home shed a tear right along with him.

"Well, I'm impressed, Jonathan. And I'm sure all of our viewers will be moved by your statements."

"Thank you, Kendall. Thank you for allowing me to share my feelings with the nation."

"You are most welcome, Jonathan. Truly." Kendall turned to face the camera. "OK. We'll take a short break, but we'll be right back, when I'll be making Earth-based fish cakes with Jonathan right here in Cell number 247 and Nigel-666 will be playing live in the prison canteen singing his new hit 'Interstellar Incarceration' from his new film "Jailstation Rock". So, don't go away!"

\*

Across town, Budgie, Jonathan's ex-partner-in-crime, was washing dishes in a restaurant chain, celebrity chef Rock Stein's 'Dishes From Fishes'. He was, ironically, hosing off a plate of crabcakes, and watching the TV at the same time. Now, Budgie was no multi-tasker, and his apron was getting soaked as he watched Kendall Crisp, but he was oblivious to his error, so absorbed was he by the

109

interview on Channel 11.

"Hey-a, Budgie, what's it with-a you?" It was Poncho Di Marte, head chef of the restaurant. "You get-a back to work! Or I tell-a probation officer you no-a work-a hard, you a lazy TV watcher, comprende?"

"Yes, chef, I hear. I get back to work, OK." It was then that he noticed his apron was drenched in water and his clothes underneath were sodden. "Oh, shizz, Jon-7, look what you've made me do!" And at that moment, something very, very strange happened...

A chemical alteration took place in Budgie's brain, the cause of which was unknown to Budgie (he only felt a slight loosening of something inside his head that made him shake it a few times) but was actually the industrial strength washing-up liquid he'd been passively inhaling for the last few weeks. Some neurological fibre had moved, or wriggled, or scrabbled its way from one part of his cerebral cortex to another, taking with it the last remnants of submissive thought. Somewhere along the line they'd dissolved into nothingness and Budgie's seemingly inbuilt instinct to obey others finally took leave of his mind.

Budgie shook his head again, furiously this time.

When he'd stopped that, he realised that his feelings of resentment towards Jon-7 were at an all-time high. He reflected on the many years of his life he'd wasted in servitude. So much time spent helping Jon-7. And to what end?

Budgie looked down at the sink. The water had lost all of its suds and was now a greasy bowl of greyish-brown water, with bits of fat and oil floating on top. He would've seen it was a metaphor for his own existence, had he known what that word meant, but nevertheless he certainly got the gist.

"This sink is like my life," he said. "And all because of Jon-shizzing-7. What a complete shizz!" he exclaimed. "What a total drainer! What a hoodwinking, jive-butt, loser!"

And right then and there, Budgie promised himself that he would get his revenge on Jonathan Potts, or whoever Jon-7 was pretending to be now.

All he needed was a way to do it. All Budgie needed

110

was 'a plan'.

But the problem was, he'd never made a plan before.

Jon-7 used to make all the decisions for them.

Budgie would simply carry them out.

Nevertheless, he pulled the plug on the sink and watched as the whirlpool began to spin the water away down the hole. And just as the column of air in the parabola was being sucked into a tornado-like pattern, so the vortex soon lead his thoughts down into a spiral of hypnotic concentration…

Budgie felt a bit lightheaded, but sailed his mental dinghy straight down the corkscrew of his mind…

*Right, then… A plan… It can't be that hard…* (his brain told him).

Budgie closed his eyes and tried to envisage where he was now (i.e. in the kitchen of 'Dishes From Fishes') and then, where he wanted to be (i.e. standing triumphantly, arms held aloft, with one foot on a prostrate Jon-7).

It seemed simple.

*Now all I need to do now is fill in the bit in the middle.*

*…*

*But with what?*

Budgie tried to concentrate. It was difficult, at first, but soon his mind's eye was full of moving pictures and imaginary words:


*He saw himself walking out of the front door of the restaurant and down the main street. He went left, right, left again, waited at the pedestrian crossing lights.*

'C'mon, c'mon. Hurry up, lights!'

*Went down several more streets and a few more crossings, until he arrived at the Muhaze Penetentiary.*

'Hey, this is going better than I expected!'

*He walked through the station entrance and up to the front desk. Behind it sat a woman with big hair and a uniform. Budgie smiled to himself as he walked confidently towards her.*

'Hello, I've come to see Jonathan Potts. Cell 247,' he said.

'Sorry, no visitors allowed,' said the woman, without

111

*looking up from her paperwork. 'Jonathan Potts is by appointment only. Those are the rules.'*

*Budgie's brain hadn't seen this coming.*

*'But I've walked all this way, in my imagination, and that wasn't easy, given my capacity for hypothetical thought,' replied Budgie.*

*'I can't help you there, sir.' The guard went back to her paper shuffling.*

*The mind's eye Budgie was flummoxed...*

The real world Budgie felt his brow begin to furrow. His eyes soon narrowed with a slight feeling of pain around his frontal lobe, clearly the effort of thinking up stuff was taking its toll. Then, after a few more seconds of this, he exhaled in frustration and his mind went blank.

"Oh shizz it!" he exclaimed.

"Hey, you. Pappagallino!" It was chef Di Marte (who else would know the Earth-based Italian for 'Budgerigar'). "Get-a back to work! Stop-a daydreaming!"

But Budgie's brain had changed, remember?

"No!" he shouted. "I've had it! I quit this stinking job!"

Budgie removed his wet apron and threw it at the chef. He then stomped out of the kitchen and into the dining room, past the customers ("You know, if he drops the steaks on the floor he just rinses them off and serves them anyway."), past the cloakroom girl ("Janice, you are the most beautiful girl I know and I love you.") - and out the front door. Budgie carried on down the street, turning left, then right, then left again, waited at the crossing ("C'mon, c'mon...") down a few more streets and across a few more crossings, and finally he arrived at the penitentiary. He walked straight through the entrance, and over to the big-haired woman at the front desk.

"Hello. I've come to see Jonathan Potts. I have no appointment, but I don't care what you say, I'm going to see him right now!"

"Yes, sir. Of course. No problem. Step this way." She got up from her desk.

"You what?" replied a stunned Budgie.

"Step this way, sir. You wanted to see Mr. Potts, was that correct?"

"Um, yes. It's just that I... Well, I didn't think that you'd let me... Oh, it doesn't matter." Budgie followed the lady through to security, and as he did so, he wondered about how reality was different from just thinking about a thing, and how confusing it all was. But he also thought how he was beginning to like his *new* reality.

Now that he'd decided to believe in himself, for once.

## Chapter 22

*14:45 - 13 October, 2187 (Starship Argon, Lumiol-S3 Apex, Michael 6 Quadrant)*


As the Peers walked into the main lobby area of the Argon, flashbulbs went off temporarily blinding the young wielders. This was directly followed by loud applause and shouting coming from the Press area:

"Over here, Marcie! Smile for the camera!"

"Cy Gibson, what's it like being an ambassador?"

"Linden, where is Leylaan X?"

And so forth.

Dr. Gössner arranged the Peers in order of age on the platform and, when done, signalled to Spalding that they were ready.

Reg Spalding approached the lectern and held up his hands: "Gentlemen, ladies of the Interstellar Press. Please, no questions just yet. There will be plenty time for that after the presentation. Now, let us get on with the ceremony. Members of the press, Lieutenant McGilvary of the Argon spacecraft."

McGilvary came forward.

"Ladies and gentlemen of the press, people at home. We are here today to celebrate the initiation of these fine citizens into the IFS Interstellar Ambassador's

Programme. Seven Peers are here with us. There are three more, but their arrivals have been delayed. Let me introduce them to you now…"

The Lieutenant reeled off the names of the new ambassadors and gave details of their home planets and respective ages. The press took more photos of each Peer as they were presented, until, with the presentation of Linden, that part of the ceremony came to and end. Spalding took over from McGilvary for the next part: the reuniting of the parents with the Peers.

Just then, a member of the press called out: "But where's Holly Dreamo, Reg?"

Spalding couldn't resist answering the question. He knew the press would ask that question eventually, and was keeping Holly back for a big *Ta-da!* moment - and this was it.

Spalding grinned. "Why she's right here… Ladies and gentlemen, Miss Holly Dreamo!"

Holly appeared from a side entrance, followed by Cox and Ω.

Word of her exploits on Plaateux-5 had clearly made the rounds on the newsreels of the cosmos, because the wall of noise that erupted upon her entrance equalled that of all the Peers put together. The press called out her name and the flashes went off again in earnest.

It was the first time in weeks that the Peers had seen her, and she looked different, to them. There was a blank expression on her face that hadn't been there before. She was smiling, but it seemed like it had been stuck onto her face.

Holly walked straight over to the Peers and stood in her usual position, at the far end beside Cy. She said nothing to her friends as she passed them by.

Spalding approached the microphone, delighted with himself. "And now, the moment we have all been waiting for," slimed the IFS Übermensch, "the reunification of the Peers with their families. If you would care to turn your attention to the docking corridor on my left, you will see the arrival of the Parents of the Peers."

Through a blue curtain emblazoned with the IFS logo, the Parents of the Peers entered the lobby area.

It was a *coupe de grâce* for Spalding, and he knew it.

He beamed from ear to ear as the Peers ran to meet their relatives. There were tears of joy on both sides, and even Lead-Out found herself welling up. More photographs were taken, and throughout the cosmos people of all creeds shared in the joyous (though highly manipulative) moment.

After enough flashes to light up a small city, questions were then taken, with the Peers holding their own with the press. They gave off-the-cuff answers to the banal queries asked, and had the over-excited audience splitting their sides:

Q: "Show us an example of your powers, Cy!"
A: *"Two plus two equals four."*

*Q:* "What message have you got for people like you all over the cosmos, Ellery?"
A: *"Don't forget to turn off the cooker before you leave the house."*

Q: "Marcie, what do hope to achieve as an Ambassador?"
A: *The acceptance of all individuals regardless of colour, creed or ability... oh, and much later bedtimes for all 14 year olds."*

And so on...

Needless to say, the press lapped it up.

No questions were asked of Holly during the ceremony, the press had been under strict orders not to. Her rictus grin stayed in place the whole time, and glances were cast between the group - it was clear that the Peers thought her demeanor to be very odd, almost robotic, so devoid was it of personality.

But soon the event was over and the families retired to the Stateroom where a private meeting was to be held.

*

Marcie decided to investigate the Holly scenario. She saw her chance as Holly's parents, looking weary with the weight of their daughter's predicament, were engaged in

116

conversation with Reg Spalding.

"Hi, Holly. How are you?" she said, walking over to her.

Holly looked up: "I'm very well, Marcie. How are you?"

"Yeah, great. How are your folks?"

"They're very well, thank you. And yours?"

"Terrific, thanks, yeah." Marcie detected wierdness, in large quantities. She decided to mix things up a bit.

"Nice weather we're having, huh?"

"Marvellous weather," replied Holly.

"And we're all so happy to be ambassador's, aren't we?"

"Yes, we are so privileged to serve the IFS, in any way that we can."

"I love puppies and bunnies, don't you?"

"Oh yes, puppies and bunnies are my favourites."

"And sharks, they are the best."

"Sharks are amazing."

"And Earth-based brussel-sprouts, they're delicious, don't you think?"

"Oh yes, and so nutritious."

"Yeah... Well, listen, it's been great talking to you, Holly. See you later."

"Yes. I will look forward to that," replied Holly, then turned away to look at the stars again.

Marcie could see Linden had been listening in on their conversation - she went over to him.

"Well, what do you think?"

"I think Holly is a brand new person."

"Yep, looks like it. Sounds like it too. Did you notice all her answers are positive. 'No negativity has been tolerated'. Who does that remind you of, Linden?"

Linden smiled. "Old comb-over himself."

"Correct in one."

"A meeting is called for, I think."

"Yes, but without Little Miss Happiness here."

"I agree."

But the reunion was all too brief. And soon Spalding was eagerly ushering the parents back onto the Turandot, and the Peers back into the Holdings area.

"You will see your parents again soon, Peers," he said,

cursorily. "It is the IFS's top priority that you remain in contact with them throughout your time as ambassadors."

"Our *life sentence*, I think he means," said Marcie, to Tora.

This time Spalding hadn't heard her. There was party music playing and the other Peers were talking loudly about the things they'd said to the press and the news they'd received from their parents.

Then, Lieutenant McGilvary arrived and whispered something to Spalding that made his face go dark. He left with her immediately.

Marcie, on seeing this, turned to Linden. "Five minutes, your room?"

Linden nodded. "Great, tell the others. But listen, we've not got much time. We must act quickly."

Marcie nodded and went round the others with the plan.

After telling everyone, she looked over at Holly and saw her staring out of a small porthole window at the stars, still smiling that strange fixed smile. She left her to her positive thoughts, or whatever was going on in her troubled mind.

If indeed it was *her* mind.

## Chapter 23
*14:47 - 13 October, 2187 (Muhaze, Tapi-36)*


After Jon-7s emotional plea to the nation, calls had been coming into the Prison from Tapians asking for his release.

How short a memory span did they have?

Had they already forgotten what Jon-7 had done?

Either way, by the time Budgie got through security and up to cell 247, Kendall was already making the fishcakes.

"What's going on?" asked Budgie, tapping the shoulder of a man with cabling wrapped around his arm.

"Crab-cakes," replied the technician.

"Hey! Watch your language, pal," said Budgie.

"No. They're *making* crab-cakes. Kendall and Jonathan, on TV. This is 'Late Lunch With Kendall Crisp'." Then a flash of recognition came across the fellow's face. "Hey, aren't you 'what's his name'? Jonathan's buddy. Um... Bald Eagle... no, Barn Owl... no, wait a minute... it begins with a 'B', I'm sure of it... Blue Jay?"

Budgie shook his head.

"Oh, what is it...? Hang on... I've got it! Budgie! You're Budgie, aren't you? Jonathan Potts' old sidekick! Hey everybody! Look, it's Budgie! Jonathan's friend!"


119

The TV crew stopped what they were doing and crowded around the diminutive scally, who by this time was protesting: "No, I'm not him. I'm not Budgie. Please, leave me alone."

But it was too late. A makeup crew was already thrusting a powder puff into his face, and being shuffled over to Jon-7's cell.

The show's director, Tristan Hughes-Kitsch, was motioning to Kendall, who rather unprofessionally, had just taken a big bite of crabcake.

Hughes-Kitsch mouthed the words: 'It's Budgie. Interview him,' at Crisp.

Kendall shook his head. "Mm-muufflumph-ifff-fuulmmph-oaaf-craaaphcaaffph" he said.

Hughes-Kitsch mouthed back: 'Just do it!'

Jon-7 saw his old comrade. "Ah-ha! Budgie, my old fruit. You've come to rescue me, have you?"

Budgie hesitated for a second, then said: "Not a chance, *Jonathan Potts*." Budgie said his name like he was eating a huge slice of lemon.

Jon-7 was taken aback. "Oh come, come, great chum. A changed man am I. Surely you can see that? Check out the prisoner hair, eh? And the duds?"

"No. You're still the same old Jon-7 that I knew. The same guy who was a leader of an absolutely rubbish terrorist group, the same paid up employee of TAPCON, the same fixer of elections and printer of illegal currencies, the same no good, dirty-rotten -"

"OK, Budge. Enough's enough, my fruity cake."

Budgie was about to carry on, when something very strange happened:

The window at the far end of the prison hallway smashed through! And in came the Froome on grappling hooks!

Now, this would seem like a very Deus Ex Machina moment, but, no.

You see, earlier that day the Froome had held a meeting - one that had begun with a lot of shouting.

It was Grisshum doing the shouting, of course...

\*

"Right then! Everybody simmer down! We are gathered

120

here to finalise our plans for project 'Revenge'. Jon-7 still owes us. He owes us *big-time*. He sold us out. He double-crossed us!"

The Froome all went: 'Yeah!', 'Darn Tootin' and so forth.

Grisshum continued: "We know that Jon-7 is being held in the Muhaze Pen. So we're going to swing in there, literally, and get him out. Then we're going to make him give us what we want!"

Again, the Froome voiced their approval.

"And what *is* that?" asked Grisshum, of his followers.

The Froome turned and looked at each other. They shrugged their shoulders, and generally looked very confused indeed.

Grisshum asked again: "I said... And what *is* that?"

There was silence again, until Baloney Tire spoke up. "We don't know, Grisshum. What *is* it?"

Grisshum was about to speak when he realised that he didn't know either. "Um, oh fire, I've forgotten..."

\*

But nevertheless, there they were now, crashing through the oriel window of Muhaze Penitentiary's second floor cell-block.

The cameras spun round, the TV people shrieked, Jon-7 swore several times, and Budgie smiled like a child.

"Keep rolling!" bawled Tristan Hughes-Kitsch.

The Froome ran down the hallway like a badly-drilled SWAT team, but everyone hurriedly got out of their way, despite appearances. They were down at Jon-7's cell in literally minutes.

"Buzz-Blades at the ready, Bardroola!" shouted Grisshum.

"Gotcha' Grissh! C'mon' Lapwing!" Bardroola and Lapwing revved up their newfangled chainsaws and set to on the bars.

Kendall Crisp shrieked like a baby.

Jon-7 stood by, watching, nonplussed He was used to the lunacy of The Froome. Because usually he was the cause of it.

"Are you getting all this?" said Tristan Hughes-Kitsch

121

to his cameraman.

"Yes, boss. Getting it all."

Budgie was still smiling. It was like all his Herramases had come at once. Here he was, having only a few minutes ago tried to make a plan of his own, and now it was turning out even better than he ever could have expected. He watched on, as Grisshum took control of the broadcast.

"Hey! You! Director man! Come here!"

Tristan Hughes-Kitsch was livid. "How dare you! How draining dare you come in here and ruin my programme?"

"I'll ruin you if you're not careful," retorted Grisshum.

Tristan gave him an astonished look. "Well, I've never been so insulted in all my -"

"Bardroola, a little greasing of the wheel over her, if you please, my love?"

"You bet, hun," she replied, and began to rev up her Buzz-Blade whilst walking towards Tristan Hughes-Kitsch with a slightly evil, yet gleeful, look on her face.

"Ah," said the TV tyke. "I completely understand you, now." He turned to Grisshum with a nervy smile. "So, how can I be of help?"

"That's better," said Grisshum. "I'm glad you've seen the light. Bardroola, call off the dogs."

"As you wish, sweets," she said, turning off her DIY destroyer.

"So, are you still rolling?"

"Yes, we are."

"And this is going out live?"

"Indeed, to the whole planet."

"Hey. Cool."

"Yes, it is rather *cool*, isn't it?" said Hughes-Kitsch, looking pleased with himself.

Grisshum went over to Kendall and grabbed the host's microphone. Then came back over to the camera. He looked straight into the lens: "People of Tapi-36," he began. "We're very sorry to interrupt this programme, but you see, Mr. Potts over there owes us. In fact, I've just remembered what it was he promised us. A moon. Kloq-888 to be exact. And we're here to get it from him. Unfortunately, he doesn't seem to have it on his person.

So we need to take him with us to see President Swish. Awfully sorry for the interruption. We do hope this doesn't ruin your crab cakes."

Grisshum dropped the mic onto the floor. "C'mon Froome. Let's get out of here! And bring the swine... sorry, bring Mr. Potts, if you please."

And with that, Grisshum and the Froome swung themsleves back out of the prison and down onto their truck waiting outside.

Kendall Crisp looked at his director.

Hughes-Kitsch sighed. "I think that's a wrap, people."

# Chapter 24
*15:15 - 13 October, 2187 (Starship Argon, Lumiol-S3 Apex, Michael 6 Quadrant)*


"And so you see, President Swish, the power station will be perfectly safe. I can guarantee the IFS will put all necessary safety precautions into place and there will be no issues with having the plant so near to Muhaze City."

"That is a very bold promise, Mr. Spalding. Are you sure you can keep it?" replied Janeee.

"100%, President Swish."

"Captain Jameson and I have been discussing -"

Spalding cut her short. "It is of no consequence what Captain Jameson's views are in this matter. The orders have already been given. We are here only as protocol demands it. Although we do not expect you to roll over on this matter, we do expect you to fully support it."

"I see," said Janeee. "That is the situation, is it?"

"It is."

Janeee sighed. She was quickly realising that her new job was not all she thought it would be. She felt like her hands were tied in several matters; that she was a puppet to the higher bureaucracy that pulled the strings, and now she was being forced to compromise her beliefs. What could she do? Stamp her feet? Scream and shout?

"Very well. But I would like to be informed of developments on all fronts, as they reveal themselves, Mr. Spalding."

"Of course, President Swish," said Reg. "I will see to it personally that updates are sent to you daily."

"Thank you. Now if you'll excuse me, I have some urgent business to attend to."

"Ah, David Sempre. Most annoying, him returning like this."

"Yes," replied Janeee. "And I would hope the IFS is looking into the issue at their end?"

"Oh yes, I spoke to Commander Samms only moments ago. They are well on their way to sending some intelligence to your people, I gather."

"Thank you, Mr. Spalding. That is helpful."

"Good day, President... I'll talk to you later, Jameson."

Janeee's screen went to snow.

A buzz came on her intercom. It was Milksilk.

"Miss President, we have word on the Sempre case. They're holding a youth downtown. A Kané Smith. Brother of Mikita. History of drug issues, arson etc."

Janeee looked at Jameson. "I'll be right there, thank you, Captain."

*

"We must be quick everyone, there's no telling when Spalding will be back," said Linden.

"Yeah, to haunt us with his weird hair," quipped Marcie.

"Do you want someone to keep watch?" asked Cy. "Because I'll go do it if you want?"

Linden pushed his specs. "Cy, if you don't want to do this then that is fine with all of us. Sometime in the future you may want to, but for us, well, there is no decision, we want to be rid of the GC. It causes too many problems and - well, you know the reasons. I shan't repeat them."

Cy took a deep breath. "No, you're right. If I didn't have the GC then I could go home, couldn't I? The IFS wouldn't need me and I could go home with my mum and dad, don't you think?"

125

"I think that would happen eventually, yes. Probably sooner than we think once the IFS find out what we've done."

Cy smiled. "Then, I'm in."

"You sure?" asked Marcie.

"100%," replied Cy.

"OK. That's all of us… Let's begin."

The Peers closed their eyes.

"Engage."


It only took them a minute or so to get through the Crossing Point and on into Sanctuary.

They passed quickly through, and on towards the central emission point.

~ There it is, ~ said Linden, as the ground below slowly began to shift. ~ Go carefully, Peers. ~

The Peers moved slowly and quietly, but soon the tremor became worse and was buffeting the Peers left and right, backwards and forwards.

~ It's too much! ~ exclaimed Tora. ~ I can't concentrate with all this movement! ~

~ You've got to try, Tora! ~ shouted Marcie. ~ We've all got to do this together! ~

Linden cut to the chase. ~ Picture getting rid of your powers in your minds and send it down to the source. Let's do it. Now! ~

To the Peers' surprise, six, black, wraith-like swirls emanated from their foreheads. They curled around each other and wound their way towards the glowing epicentre.

~ It's working! ~ shouted Linden. ~ Keep going! Keep going! ~

But the source was not giving up without a fight. In retaliation the GC unleashed a swathe of golden light that sent the Peers sprawling backwards in pain.

~ It's fighting back at us! ~

~ Push harder, again! We must try again! ~

The Peers united once again and this time it seemed with renewed vigour. Their black swirls seemed to force the core backwards. Pushing harder the Peers saw their swirls disappear down the heart of the GC control. The shuddering ground subsided, leaving only a feeling of a soft electric current buzzing under their feet.

The Peers looked around at each other. Then said, as one:

~ Disengage. ~

They were back in Linden's room, slightly dazed but nothing more. They had no time to confer, because there in the doorway stood Holly Dreamo. Her face red with anger. Her fists clenched at her sides.

"What have you been d-d-doing?" she demanded.

Linden spoke first. "Ah, Holly. How are you?"

"Doesn't ma-matter! What have you been d-d-doing, behind my b-b-back?"

"Nothing, Holly," said Marcie. "Just talking. Are you OK? Would you like to join us?"

Holly looked at them in disbelief, she swooned slightly on her feet. "If I... If I... If I..." she stuttered, then collapsed.

Marcie turned to Linden. "Uh-oh," she said.

"Check her over," said Tora. "Look for anything weird on her, Augs, implants, anything. Something is definitely up with Miss Dreamo."

"Agreed," said Linden. "Let's be quick, we don't have much -"

"Time?" came a voice at the door.

It was Spalding.

"The word you're looking for is 'time', isn't it Mr. Hoon. And if looks are not deceiving I would venture that you Peers have precious little of the stuff left, if you continue to carry on like this."

Cy spoke up. "Mr. Spalding, Holly is unwell. She's fallen over."

"Yes, Mr. Gibson. I am aware of that, thank-you."

"Well, shouldn't you take her sick bay, sir?" he continued.

"Yes, yes, boy! All in good time!"

"I'll help you, sir?" he added.

Spalding lashed out at Cy. He struck him on the cheek leaving a red welt in the shape of his hand.

Cy cried out in pain. "Why did you do that? I was only trying to be nice."

"Quiet! I've had enough of your babbling, Gibson! All of you! Enough! Go to your rooms and don't come out until I say so!"

The Peers didn't move.

"Now!" he bellowed.

Slowly, the Peers walked to their respective quarters and closed their doors.

Spalding picked up Holly's body and removed her from the Holdings.

## Chapter 25
*15:33 - 13 October, 2187 (Muhaze, Tapi-36)*


Kané's face was a mess. He'd been in the Police holdings cell getting the shizz kicked out of him for around a half an hour. His whole body ached. His jaw worst of all.

They kept asking him the same questions over and over. But he knew nothing about Sempre, how could he give them information when he didn't know anything?

"Where's Sempre?" demanded Captain Hughes, his patience tried.

"I don't know what you're talking about," replied Kané, sternly.

BAM!

Another fist landed heavily at his jaw.

"I'll ask you again, Mr. Smith. Where is David Sempre?"

Kané lifted his sore head to the policeman, as he repeated for the umpteenth time: "I've told you, I know nothing about Sempre!"

The cop recoiled his arm ready to strike again.

But Kané's anger spilled over as he felt a sudden rush of power within himself. Deep down. Painful. Golden in colour.

Captain Hughes froze. His eyes squinted as he saw the

ochre force emitting from Kané. In an instant he was enveloped in the GC's wrath and a sharp crack in the air sent him flying into the corner of the cell.

Kané couldn't believe it. He hadn't summoned the Circuit since he was a boy. It felt dreadful, excrutiating. His body was aflame and his bones ached with an awful heat; his skin felt like it had been peeled from his body; like he'd been flayed alive. Kané screamed in agony. The GC had always been painful for Kané. But this? This was unlike any pain he had ever experienced in his life. It was too much. He fell unconscious in his chair.

Hughes wasn't badly hurt. He shook his head a couple times, dazed, as he rose to his knees. But then got to his feet, a look of extreme hatred broke across his face as he lurched towards Kané. "Why you draining son of a -"

"Wait! Stop!" came a voice from the cell door.

It was Janeee Swish, with three armed guards behind her, she'd seen  Kané using the GC. "What is going on here? What are you men doing? This is totally unacceptable!"

Hughes turned, saw Janeee and immediately stood to attention. "Yes, President Swish, of course, ma'am. My apologies, ma'am."

Janeee was already over to Kané and untying his hands. "Some humanity, please! This man is clearly unwell, look at him. He is suffering from drug withdrawal, not to mention severe concussion. He must be taken care of first and foremost, gentlemen. See to it this happens, without delay!" She turned to Hughes. "Captain, I am appalled. You are hereby relieved of duty. Go home. A tribunal date will be set for your conduct here. You other officers are docked this month's pay and will face questioning as to your involvement in this unsightful mess. Guards, take Mr. Smith to sick bay."

Janeee's guards removed Kané from the cell. His body was limp and his head hung at the neck.

"You other men, get back to work."

On Janeee's words the remaining police officers left the holding room, avoiding her gaze as they did so.

Janeee was left alone in the cell. She had witnessed Kané's use of the GC through the door hatch, and it had frightened her. She'd never seen the Golden Circuit in action. When would've she had the chance - it was rarer than rocking-horse shizz.

Was it coincidence that the boy was at Quasar's at the same time as Sempre and Polo were suspected of being there? He was a drug addict, that was clear, but was he involved somehow in Sempre's plans? She would need to handle the questioning herself.

The whole situation was dire. She felt she was losing her grip on her men and the support of her top brass. And now that Sempre's whereabouts were unknown (as if he had simply disappeared off the face of Tapi-36) she would need to act fast and with decisiveness.

She followed the guards and Kané to sick bay.

Forty-five minutes later, Kané was free.

*

Spalding had gone into overdrive. The Peers were a problem, but not one he couldn't overcome. They were up to something, that was for sure, but he'd dealt with much more difficult cases. It was simply a matter of speeding things up. Holly would need to remain onboard while the Peers would travel immediately to Tapi-36, do the TV interview then stay under close surveillance, until he was ready for them.

Ready for them to supply the energy to the new Power Station.

## Chapter 26
*15:43 - 13 October, 2187 (Grafuulen, Tapi-36)*

David Sempre woke to find himself strapped to an operating table. He immediately smelt the pungent odour of acid, or some other chemical closely related, nearby. His eyes watered at the reek of it. He pulled on his bonds, to no avail, then let loose a howl of frustration and anger that seemed to shake the large, high-ceilinged room to its foundations.

At the far end, a door opened, and through it walked the man with the spider augmentation. His footsteps echoed, as he walked slowly and methodically over to Sempre. He said nothing. In fact, he did not speak until he was directly over Sempre's face, looking down at the disabled half-man/half-woman before him.

"Mr. Sempre," he began, with a voice like fingernails on a chalkboard. "You have become even more of a nuisance than you were before. It is most annoying for us."

"Who are you? What do you want?" spat Sempre. "Are you Ramrod?"

The man smiled. "So many questions, Mr. Sempre. So many questions. But all in good time." The man paused. "I am Marcus A12."

*An A12 droid,* thought Sempre. *A droid, with shizzing*

*Augs.* "Let me go!" shouted Sempre, as he again fought with his straps, pulling his arms and legs against them.

"Save your energy, Mr. Sempre, you may need it later."

Sempre stopped his movements, then noticed his NITs had disappeared.

"NITs?!" screamed Sempre. "Sempre says 'Attack!'"

The man laughed.

Sempre looked around. "Where are the NITs? What have you done with them?"

"Do not worry, your little friends are safe. You see, we are familiar with Quince and Mitchell's work. And besides, they need their controller - i.e. your voice - in order to operate. Our lab people are very well-trained. We had few troubles containing them. They are not sentient, Mr. Sempre."

"Not like *you*, Marcus A12."

The droid smiled again. "Now. Let us begin... Mr. Sempre, meet Ramrod."

An electronic arm came up from beneath the operating table and moved towards an area above Sempre's groin. Out of the tip of the arm came a small shaft with a round, bulbous end that slowly flowered into eight claws. From this, emerged a jaw of metallic teeth, spittle dripping from the ends. They opened and closed eagerly. Sempre's face changed to one of terror. He thought he could see eyes up inside the shaft. Something in there was alive.

The man was still smiling. "Don't worry. It will not bite you... As long as you behave yourself."

Spittle from the maw in the shaft dropped onto his skin. It burned.

Sempre cried out in pain.

"Oh," said the man, "I forgot about that." It has been awhile since our last 'intruder'. But it is not *your* body, is it? So not to worry."

"Where am I?"

"You are in the IFS base on Tapi-36, Mr. Sempre. A secret holding. One of many dotted around the Quadrant." Marcus paused, again. "Ah, I see from your reaction that you are surprised, Mr. Sempre. You see, there are many things on this planet, in this galaxy, that you are unaware of. Things your father never told you about. Things your dear mother, may she rest in peace, never told you about. But then again, our dear Mayette knew nothing of the bigger plans." Marcus laughed. "You don't think we can simply rule from afar, do you Mr Sempre? That Earth is the only location we operate from? Don't be so naive -"

At that moment, through the same door that Marcus A12 had just come through came Eugene Samms, Head of the IFS. Sempre recognised him immediately.

"Samms!" cried Sempre. The beast in the metal arm made a high-pitched sound of anger at his raised voice. Sempre sensed it slithering in the tube. "What is going on here? Why am I being held like this? I'll report you to the... to the..." Sempre realised he had no one to report Samms to. He was in charge of *everything*.

"Mr. Sempre," began Samms. "Welcome to my humble abode. It's not much, but then again, Tapi-36 is our furthest outpost. But no less important for it, may I say."

"Why have you brought me here?"

Samms smiled. "We were very surprised that the Specialists rescued you in this way. Such loyalty in one's staff is very unusual, wouldn't you say?"

"Just get on with it," snarled Sempre. The thing in the metal tube was getting edgy.

"We could just kill you, you know. Right now. Be done with you for good. But you have already been seen by the good people of Tapi-36, have you not? And Janeee Swish knows you exist... then there's the police and so forth..."

Sempre could see the eyes of the beast watching him from inside the tube. He shifted uneasily.

"You see, the IFS.... Hmmmm... how shall I put this..." Samms brought both his hands up to his lips as if he were about to pray. He wasn't praying though. Not a man like Eugene Samms. He was only thinking dark thoughts. "There are many layers of control, Mr. Sempre. Everywhere you choose to look, in business, in law, in politics, in nature. All of it obeying the rules; the imposed system of hierarchies. And these things are there for a reason. The strong, the weak. Some deserve to be at the top, others find their places lower down. You, for example. Carrying out your father's work. The manual.

Remember? You let that slip, didn't you? Most unfortunate. But that was your role in the great scheme of things, following in Sashan's footsteps. Do you see what I mean?"

"Get to the point, Samms!"

Samms ignored him and carried on in the same tone. "Your father was a good man, David. May I call you David?" Samms didn't wait for a reply. "He was totally insane, but good for the IFS. You would have done well to heed his example a bit more. And it was unfortunate that the GC wielders meddled in our business, albeit unknowingly. However, it won't be long now before we have them all. But *this? This* is unexpected. You, simply turning up here unannounced, as it were. It's all very... *inconvenient*. Therefore, Mr. Sempre, I have no option but to place you under surveillance, until I can think of a use for you." Samms gestured at the android. "Marcus, take him to the holding rooms."

Samms turned and left the theatre.

Marcus A12 grinned to himself, and pressed a button that caused Ramrod's tube to retract. Sempre breathed a sigh of relief, but soon his anger returned as he replayed what Samms had just said:

*Inconvenient?* he said, to himself. *I'll show him how inconvenient I can be...*

# Chapter 27
*15:55 - 13 October, 2187 (Muhaze, Tapi-36)*

Gompi and Charly were busy at their apartment. They were finishing off decorating the new arrival's bedroom. Gompi was just putting the last touch of blue gloss to the window sill, and Charly was laying out the bed linen on the cot.

"I disappointed Dr. Tam couldn't help us," said Gompi.

"Yes, me too. But he right. Janeee Swish will sort."

Gompi nodded and smiled. He wasn't so sure, but he didn't say so.

"I very excited, Gompi," said Charly. "I can't wait to see what little Gompi look like."

"Yes, me too," said Gompi. "They say he will look like half of me, and half of you. They programme the computers to make him exactly half and half. But one thing for sure... he have sliver hair!"

"You right, Gompi," replied Charly. "And he be nice and kind, don't you think?"

"Oh yes, because you kind, Charly."

"And you are kindest mutant I ever know," said Charly.

Gompi smiled. Then, after a few seconds, said: "There! I all done!" and put his brush into the thinners.

136

"Me too," said Charly, putting a little blue pillow at the head of the bed.

They both stood back to admire the room. It was beautifully done. A mobile hung over the cot with Earth-based rockets and stars hanging down. A fresh smell of lavender filled the air and the lights were dimly lit in anticipation of the newly-made.

Tomorrow they would go and pick him up from the Clinic.

Tomorrow they would be a family.

\*

Back at the underground lab, Tamashito had problems. The network had been so badly destroyed in the Froome Skirmish that many of the chains between systems had been severed. He needed to find a way of transmitting the data to the mutants using untried methods. He knew there was a way to do it, he just couldn't work out how he was going to achieve it. His brow broke out in a sweat, and his fingers searched the keyboard for the correct buttons. Power was intermittent and several times he needed to begin again from scratch after the computer crashed. He eventually managed to rig up a power source that was reliable and this had given him a renewed confidence. The transmitter at Sennon Point was still functional, but he had to hack into the system to turn it back on after the PASIV's last visit. He had time, but not much. He needed to work faster.

# Chapter 28
*16:02 - 13 October, 2187 (Grafuulen, Tapi-36)*


"So, Miss Smith, it appears that we have come to a rather annoying lull in the proceedings," said David Sempre.

Polo sat on a chair - one of two, in the bare, white-walled secure room - hand on chin, deep in thought. Sempre paced the length of the floor.

"Can you stop with the mad-lion in an Earth-based zoo business, please?" she retorted. "It's making me nervous."

Sempre stopped. "My humbles, Miss. Smith." He went and sat in the other chair. "I'm not quite myself today."

Polo looked at Sempre and found he was smiling. She began to laugh dryly. "You're telling me," she replied.

Sempre's personality had changed over the course of the last hour or so. He'd become calmer. Much less of a lunatic. His face had begun to change, too. It was softer, as if the female part of him was beginning to take over; like the feminine side was becoming the dominant one. It was very weird.

"We must remove ourselves from out of this predicament, Miss Smith."

"And how do you propose we do that? There are guards all over the place. And we have no idea where 'out' is."

"Yes, you have a point there," Sempre paused, then out of the blue asked: "Why do you wear suits, Miss Smith? Is it that you want to be a man?"

Polo laughed. "That's rich, coming from you. Given your current condition."

Sempre smiled again. Twice in the space of 20 seconds. This was a new record for him.

Polo shook her head. "No. I don't want to be a man," she replied. "I don't want to be anything. Just myself. I just want to feel comfortable in my own skin. You must understand that."

"Oh, all too well, Miss Smith. But please, carry on."

"There's nothing more to say, really. Life goes on. I do my best to ignore people's prejudices. It's hard, but... It used to bother me, the way they looked at me, but now I don't care. It's their problem, not mine. I was made this way, deal with it."

"Very good. You are quite right. I wish I was more like you. But I wasn't made this way." He looked down at his mother's body. "So you can see how keen I am to get myself -"

Suddenly, Sempre's face went Earth-based beetroot red.

He fell from his chair, buckled over in pain.

"My chest, Miss Smith! I can't feel my -" his head fell back, blood seeped from his neck stitches.

He lost consciousness.

Polo immediately got up and banged on the door of the cell. "Guard! Guard! Something's wrong with Sempre! Open up! For Herra's sake!"

Two armed guards burst through the door, their guns aimed at Polo. "What's going on here, Miss Smith? What have you done?"

"Done? I've not done anything, you fools! It's him! He collapsed and then blood started coming out of his neck!"

The guard hit the red emergency button on the wall by the door and alarms went off. "We need to get him to the lab!"

The two guards each grabbed an arm and hoisted Sempre up off the ground. Polo began to follow them out, covering her ears with the noise.

"No, you stay here," said one of them, pushing her

139

back into the cell and shutting the door on her.


Polo watched through the glass peek hole, as the guards took Sempre towards the lift down the hall. A trail of blood marked their progress. They disappeared into the lift and Polo was left alone.

# Chapter 29
*16:10 - 13 October, 2187 (Muhaze, Tapi-36)*

The Sellihca had arrived at Muhaze City Airport, on the Western outskirts of the city. The Codes resigned themselves to Tapi-36 protocol and allowed for a transporter craft to come up to collect their passenger without the starship landing on foreign soil. Though relations between the two sides had improved since the Krashaon's appearance to bring the final Froome attack to an end, there were still boxes to be ticked as far as bringing in a civilian from another planet went, no matter who they were. Mikita said goodbye to Garthh and the crew and wistfully stepped aboard the Muhaze transporter.

She felt sad, but reassured herself that this was the right thing to do. She held Marta in her arms. Mikita wanted to leave the airport quickly and without fuss. Marta needed to be contained in order for that to happen.

The handover was quick and she was through security in no time. Several people recognised the two of them on her passage through the airport, but she tried to avoid eye contact as much as possible.

Once outside she hailed a taxi and asked the driver to take her to Harajuku Stratis on the south side, the street where Polo lived. Mikita no longer had her flat, so Polo's was the only place she could go.

Mikita sat in the back and tried to avoid the gaze of the driver in his mirror. He looked back at her several times, and she was just waiting for the moment when...

"Sorry, I have to ask," said the driver, "Are you? You know... *her?*

Mikita shook her head. "No."

"Yes, you are *her.* You're Mikita Smith, aren't you. I've seen you on the megatrons. You saved the planet, didn't you. From the Froome and that Jon-7 character. It is you, isn't it?"

"No. I'm afraid your mistaken, sir. I'm not Mikita Smith."

"Oh, come on, now. Don't be shy. You killed David Sempre, didn't you?"

"What? I did nothing of the sort!"

"A-ha! Got you!"

Mikita let out a sigh. "Yes, alright. I'm *her.*"

"I knew it! I knew it!"

"Please," said Mikita. "I'm just back from a long trip. I'm very tired and I'd appreciate it if you wouldn't -"

"Oh, a trip, you say? Where did you go? Anywhere nice?"

"No. Nowhere nice."

"Well, it must have been better than here. What with all the David Sempre business and your cousin being kidnapped. Is that why you're back?"

Mikita felt an icy chill pass through her body. She leant forward: "You what? What did you just say?"

"David Sempre's back. Didn't you know? It's all over the news, Mikita. Can I call you Mikita?"

Mikita ignored his request. "Sempre's back? But how? He's dead!"

"Nah. He's alive. Very much alive. But a bit weird looking. Death obviously wasn't that good for his health. Ha-ha!"

"And what did you say about my cousin? She's been kidnapped?"

"Yeah. The one that looks like a man. Oh, sorry. I mean the one that dresses in suits and what-not. Polo, she's called, right?"

"Yes, but where is she? Is she alright?"

"Last seen headed for Grafuulen in a chopper with

Sempre, according to the TV. But nobody's clocked them since then. They just disappeared. Janeee Swish is on to it, though. Didn't think much of her to begin with, but she's OK in my book. Here, speaking of celebs, I had that Nigel 666 in the back of my cab the other day. Herra, what a waste of outer space. Do you know what he said? He says to me -"

The driver continued his burbling while Mikita pulled herself together.

*Out of the Earth-based frying pan and into the fire...*

Five minutes later they were at Polo's. The driver hadn't stopped talking all the way there.

"How much do I owe you?"

"Nothing, love. It's on me," he said, pulling into the curb. "Consider it a debt paid."

It was just as well, as Mikita had only realised she had no money. "Oh, thanks very much. That's very kind of you."

She got out of the cab as the driver rolled down his window. "'Ere, don't go getting yourself into any more trouble now," he said, and was off into the traffic.


There was a light on in Polo's flat.

Mikita buzzed her apartment, No.6.

There was no reply.

She buzzed again.

Still nothing.

She decided to hold the buzzer down until someone answered.

After 30 seconds of this, a voice came over the speaker.

"Who is this? Go away!"

Mikita recognised the voice as her brother's. "Kané? Wait, Kané! It's me, Mikita!"

There was a short pause, before the reply.

"Mikita?"

"Yes, Kané. Open up."

The door clicked open.

Mikita walked into the lower hall. Polo's flat was on the first floor. She climbed the flight of stairs, and found Polo's door ajar.

"Kané?" said Mikita, pushing the door, cautiously.

"I'm in here."

The voice came from the living room.

Mikita went through to the front room and found Kané with a steak on his face watching TV. The news was showing the re-run footage from Paradi Square.

"What are you doing back? Not work out with your boyfriend?"

"No, Kané. It didn't. What happened to you? You look awful? Who did this to you? And Where's Polo? Taxi driver said she's been taken hostage? By Sempre."

"Yep. Thats' about correct, I'd say. On all accounts." He gestured towards his swollen eye. Courtesy of Janeee Swish's police force."

"So why are you here? Sitting watching TV? Didn't you think to go and find her?"

"Ummm... No, not really."

"For Herra's sake, Kané!"

Kané rolled his eyes.

Mikita sat down in a chair and took out her Comms device made by Marcie. She turned on the small screen and pressed the space bar on the keypad to release it from sleep mode. She scrolled through for the connect to Polo's machine. Mikita pressed ACTIVE on the touch screen and the sound came on.

"Polo? Polo, can you hear me?"

Suddenly, the screen flickered to white noise, then went blank.

Mikita pressed ACTIVE again.

Nothing.

"Polo, are you there?"

She pressed the button several times, in frustration.

Still, nothing.

"Polo? Polo, can you hear me?"

Zilch.

Mikita hit the ACTIVE key again, much harder this time.

The machine cracked at the sides and its innards sprang out onto the table.

"Oops," said Kané, flippantly.

"Kané, why are you such a scuzzball?"

"Takes one to know one, sis."

"Grow up, shizz-head. Your cousin's in trouble. So what are we going to do?"

"I dunno, Mikita. Tell your *dad*?"

"Very funny. The Argon's gone. It went two days ago. Shall I get you to burn down the house so we can send smoke signals to it?"

"Very good, Miki. You know that it wasn't me."

"Oh yeah? Who was it then?" she replied, accusingly.

"I have no idea. TAPCON, probably. She was a threat to them. But they got to her eventually, didn't they? In the end."

Mikita looked at her brother. "Yeah, I guess they did…"

There was a short silence, before Mikita spoke. "Kané?"

Kané shook his head, he recognised her tone of voice. This was the one she used to get him to something for her.

"Oh no, I don't like the sound of this."

"You're right, you won't.

"Go on, then…"

"Your GC stuff…"

"Yeah… what of it?"

"Can you use it? Properly, I mean?"

"Yes… that's how I go this shiner. Why?"

"I don't know… Can't we combine forces somehow?"

Kané was getting annoyed again. "Mikita. She's somewhere up in the air in a helicopter with a complete psychopath. No, I can't help her. She's on her own."

"Don't you want to help your cousin?"

Kané didn't reply.

"Kané, she's family!"

"Family? Why would I want to help my family? People who have basically hated and distrusted me for most of my life? People who ignored me all the time we were at TAPCON Kids. Never believed me when I said I was telling the truth about the fire. None of you. None of you believed me, Mikita. Imagine that, would you?"

"OK, OK. I get your point. But when are you going to face up to reality?"

Kané shut his eyes.

In the quiet, the TV commentary continued: "And now

145

live in the studio we have the Peers from Plaateux-5, ambassadors of the IFS…"

"Hey, turn that up."

Kané flicked the remote at the screen.

"…In a ceremony on the starship Argon, where they met up with their parents for an emotional reunion."

"That's them!" said Mikita. "That's my friends from Plaateux-5! Kané they're on TV!"

"Yeah, so what?"

Mikita had no time to answer as the door to Polo's flat burst open, and in came five armed men. Their uniforms were those of the IFS Special Guard.

The man in front flipped his visor. "Mikita Smith? Kané Smith? Please come with us."

Mikita looked at Kané.

Kané returned a worried look. "Oh no, not again…"

Together they engaged, and produced a yellow beam that was almost white in its heat. They both made a throwing motion and sent their wielding across the room. All five men were blown backwards with great force, each one crashing into the wall behind them, then collapsing unconscious on the floor.

Kané was in great pain from using the GC. "Did we kill them, Miki?"

Mikita shook her head. "No. I made sure that the force was not too strong. But I had to calm yours down a bit." She smiled at her brother. "Still got it, then eh?"

Kané half-smiled back at her. "Guess so," he replied.

146

## Chapter 30
*16:20 - 13 October, 2187 (Grafuulen, Tapi-36)*


"I knew Quince and Mitchell, Commander. Their work was highly sophisticated, they were mavericks. A word bandied about these days, but with them it's a correct fit."

The Head surgeon of the IFS, Tony Trident, was speaking with Samms via Redgum connection. The Commander was in the control room watching Trident perform the operation.

"There is nothing here of great complexity, except for the venegrafting of man to woman. I have a good idea what they did, from what is left here of their original work. Though I cannot guarantee success. I have a feeling that the healing process needed to be longer than what Mr. Sempre has undergone. And the result of that is why we are here now."

"Will he survive?" asked Samms.

"Oh, yes. In fact, he'll be on his feet by tonight."

"Tonight? But how can that be? You said he needed a longer recovery period?"

"Ah, that would be with the Specialists' healing method. Ours is far in advance of what they have. Remember, Commander, we keep the best technology for ourselves."

"Indeed, Mr. Trident." Samms smiled, and got up to

147

leave. "I will talk with you later."

"As you wish, sir," replied the surgeon. Trident turned to his assistant. "Almost done, can I trust you to finish up here, Browning?"

"Yes, of course, Dr. Trident. I reckon a few stitches are well within my capabilities, sir."

"Excellent," replied Trident - he'd not noticed the sarcasm in Browning's answer - then handed over his instruments to his junior and made his way to the clean-up room, removing his mask as he went.

Dr. Sarah Browning was Trident's latest protegé. She was ambitious and single-minded, and knew that in this day and age a woman needed to be 10 times better than a man in order to succeed at the highest level. She had climbed the IFS ladder with speed and was now ready to get what, in her mind, she deserved. That being, Tony Trident's job.

*Stitches! That's all the old swine leaves me, shizzing stitches!* She moaned to herself. *It's like he does these things on purpose. Like he's trying to humiliate me by giving me the simplest possible tasks.*

In her temper, Browning had begun sewing up Sempre's neck in a rather aggressive manner. Her assistant, Nurse Crow, felt she had to intervene.

"Dr. Browning, is there anything wrong, ma'am?"

"No. Why?" she retorted.

"Well, it's just that... um... the amount of force you're using, with the... um..."

Browning jumped down Crow's throat: "Are you questioning my abilities, Nurse Crow?"

"No, ma'am, I wouldn't dare to infer anything un -"

But at that moment, Nurse Crow felt a hand grip her tightly around the wrist. A hand that seemed to crush her forearm with its squeeze. She screamed in pain.

It was Sempre.

David Sempre sprung upright and brought the medical equipment attached to his body with him. Instruments went flying, electrodes sprang off his body and pulled themselves out of the machinery. The medical staff were frozen in horror.

"NITs!!" shouted Sempre. "Sempre says 'KILL!'"

After a moment, on the far wall, a series of dents began

to form on the metal door that led to the NITs holding room.

"Oh, Herra, no..." said Nurse Crow, under her breath. She screamed. "Run! Run for your lives!"

But Sempre still had hold of her arm - Nurse Crow wasn't going anywhere fast.

The pounding on the door got louder, increasing with rapidity as the NITs flocked together to penetrate the metal, seeking their master.

"Now you will all pay! With your lives!" thundered Sempre, pushing Nurse Crow to the ground. He swung off the operating table with the agility of a man half his age. He thrashed out at all in front of him, as the NITs burst through the door.

It was only a matter of seconds before Sempre and the NITs were moving on to their next bloodbath.

*

A call came through to Samms in his office, informing him of Sempre's breakout and subsequent annihilation of his staff.

"What do you mean he's unstoppable?" asked Samms, with genuine worry.

The operative replied that the NITs had been freed.

A heavy line appeared across his brow as Samms hung up and turned to Marcus A12.

"This isn't working, Marcus. We need to shut down the base and Sempre along with it. Prepare the release of the gas. And ready my craft for immediate embarkment and return to Base 4."

"Are you sure, Commander? But what about your staff? You can't just leave them here to die."

"Yes, Marcus. I can. We leave for the Turandot. It's the nearest craft. Wait... Are those damn freaks still on it?"

"Yes, sir. As far as I'm aware."

"Damn!"

"But sir, you have another problem..."

"Oh, what's that Marcus?"

The droid took out a Macklin-Bilson. "Me."

Samms reached for his Comms device, but he was too

slow. The droid had the gun at his throat and the trigger pulled before Samms' hand got anywhere near his handheld.

*

Inside Sempre's mind there was an unreal fury; like a volcano constantly erupting inside his head. Clearly, Tony Trident had botched the operation, or at least, connected something to where it shouldn't have been connected, as Sempre's re-wired personality had taken on hideous proportions - his eyes flamed, spit foamed at the corners of his mouth, his teeth bared maniacally.

The NITs attacked and attacked again - no one was spared.

Sempre began looking for Polo.

He would need her later.

She would be his bargaining tool.

*

Marcus A12 scanned the base from the screen in Samms' office. Bodies were everywhere. But this did not cause any sense of horror within the droid. He wasn't programmed for feelings or emotions.

He got a fix on Sempre's whereabouts: Corridor 19, the holdings area where Polo was jailed.

*

"NITs? Sempre says: 'Stop'."

The NITs froze in mid-air, and hovered, awaiting their next instructions. Sempre threw himself, shoulder first, at Polo's cell door. He only needed to do this once. It flew open.

Polo got up from the bench. "What the shizz has happened to you, Sempre?" she said.

"Shut up, girl. Come with me," he barked.

"Oh, someone's grouchy," she replied. "Looks like the IFS forgot to read the instructions before assembly."

Sempre did not smile at Polo's comment. Instead, he grabbed her by the arm and lead her out into the hall.

150

"Where are we going?" began Polo. "I presume it's not somewhere nice."

Sempre turned to her, wildly: "Keep your trap shut, girl, or my little friends will fix it so you never talk again."

Polo motioned that her lips were sealed.

Following the signs for the transport zone, Sempre and Polo were soon at the main vehicle depository. The alarms in the building had warned the staff there of a disturbance within the compound, but they were completely unprepared for what was about to befall them. Sempre and Polo burst through the double doors of the Zone.

Sempre scanned the area: "NITs? Sempre says: 'KILL!'"

Polo looked at Sempre in surprise. Then watched as the NITs flew in a grotesque swarm towards the IFS personnel. They stood transfixed by the onslaught.

"Oh, Herra..." she said, quietly, then looked away from the massacre that had begun.

"Don't be so squeamish, girl. There is plenty more of this to come."

Sempre sacnned the zone and saw that there was a military style chopper docked in a bay outside.

Polo followed his gaze. "Oh no, not another helicopter," she groaned.

Sempre looked at her with hatred. "One more word from you, girl and you will DIE! Do you understand?"

Polo nodded.

*

Marcus A12 was back in Samms' office radioing the man in the dark suit and glasses. He was ready for further orders.

"My work is done here. Is there anything else?" he said.

The reply came back in the negative.

And then, Marcus A12 exploded.

## Chapter 31
*16:34 - 13 October, 2187 (Muhaze, Tapi-36)*

Finally, Dr. Tamashito sat back in his chair and admired his work.

The code was complete.

He pressed the return key on his keyboard and waited.

After the beach ball cursor had swirled around his desktop for a few seconds the reply came: UPDATE SUCCESSFUL.

He smiled, then picked up his belongings and left the underground chamber. He would manage the school run after all.

*

On Harriet Honeste's command the Peers reeled of their names, ages and home planets. Harriet then looked around the group for someone to answer her first question. She chose Marcie.

"So tell me, Marcie," began Harriet. "What's it like being an IFS Ambassador?"

"It's OK…"

"Just 'OK'?" replied Harriet.

"Well, to tell you the truth, Harriet. It's all been a bit of a waste of time."

Harriet was intrigued "Waste of time?" she repeated.

"In what way, Marcie?"

"Well, things have changed a lot in the past while."

"Of course they have, you've become ambassadors for the -"

"No, no. That's not what I mean."

"Then what is it? Tell us. Tell Tapi-36 what's on your mind, Marcie."

"Well, you see, we don't have the Golden Circuit powers anymore."

Harriet was stupified. "You what? Don't have the Golden powers? Well, who does?"

Marcie laughed. "No one. At least, not us. Not anymore."

Harriet's mouth was wide open. She turned to Phinn. He was slack-jawed as usual.

Off stage, Reg Spalding was confused. And suddenly enraged. He walked toward the news-desk set fuming. "Stop! Stop the interview! What is the meaning of this Peers? What have you done to yourselves? Peers, come with me! Everyone come with me! This will not be broadcast!"

"No!" said Cy. "We're not coming with you!"

"Oh, yes you are young man!" shouted Spalding.

"Oh, no we're not!" shouted the Peers.

"C'mon, let's get out of here!" shouted Marcie.

The Peers ran out off the set and back the way they had come into the TV studios. Spalding followed after them.

Harriet covered for the speechless Phinn: "And that concludes our interview with the Peers. But we have a flash bulletin.... Just coming in... It appears that a rogue helicopter has left Grafuulen, presumed to be carrying David Sempre and Polo Smith, cousin of Mikita Smith. We'll have more when we come back after this message."

# Chapter 32
*16:44 - 13 October, 2187 (Grafuulen, Tapi-36)*

Sempre and Polo sat in silence as they flew over the city of Grafuulen.

Sempre was still in the operating clothes he'd had been dressed in by the nurses at the IFS bolt-hole. Except now they were heavily bloodstained. His whole body was covered in blood, making him look like some beast that had risen up from below and come to wreak havoc on the whole world above. The irony was, this is *exactly* what had occured.

Polo broke the silence between them.

"What are you going to do now, Sempre?" she asked.

"I have a plan," grumbled Sempre.

"Care to share it with me?"

"You might not want to hear it, as it probably ends with your death."

Polo gritted her teeth. "Well, if I'm going to die, perhaps I have the right to know how it's going to happen?"

"You're my hostage, I make demands, they give them to me. Simple."

"And what demands have you got in mind? Give me back my presidency Janeee or I'll kill the girl? Do you think they'll do that? Do you think they'll just roll over and let you start from where you left off?"

Sempre was silent for a second. "What other choice do I have, Miss Smith?"

"Give yourself up."

"You're as mad as I thought."

"No, seriously. Surrender. They'll put you back together. Tamashito can do it."

"Tamashito is to <u>blame</u> for all this!"

"What do you mean?"

"It was him that did this to me!" The chopper was bouncing around in the sky as Sempre's anger increased. But Polo kept on at him.

"I thought it was the Specialists?"

"No. Before that. Tamashito tricked me. He killed my father then knocked me out - pushed me into the cryro pod. After that, I don't remember. Somehow I ended up in the Specialists bunker at the Airfield. They must have taken me there after the TAPCON Tower collapsed. Herra knows how…"

Polo could see there was no point in continuing asking Sempre questions. Besides, they were already at the outskirts of Muhaze.

"We'll land on the monument in Paradi Square." Sempre nosed the chopper towards downtown. "I'm sorry Miss Smith. I had begun to like you. I am sorry this could be the end for you, but such is life… and death."

## Chapter 33
*16:46 - 13 October, 2187 (Muhaze, Tapi-36)*


Mikita and Kané left Polo's flat. To their surprise, they noticed that all the mutants were leaving their posts and heading into town. Mikita recognised the way in which they were moving. She'd seen first hand what happened when there was a change in their code programming - in the Laundry Room of the Shopping Mall when she was on the run from TAPCON. She'd outwitted enough of them during the Froome skirmish to recognise the signs - spinning eyes, a fixed gaze. She also knew that the only person who could do this to the mutants was Dr Tamashito. He was the only one with the ability. So, clearly, Dr. Tam was involved somehow with whatever had befallen Sempre and Polo. She explained as much to Kané, and together they decided to follow the mutants as they headed towards the heart of the city.

After they had walked awhile, Kané turned to his sister. "Miki?"

"Yeah?"

"You're right. I'm a shizz. I know it."

Mikita smiled. "You really didn't start that fire did you, Kané?"

Kané shook his head. "I'm guilty of many things, Mikita. But not that."

"Then I am sorry, too."

Kané nodded. "I accept your apology. Now, let's go get our cousin."

Soon they had passed the Sashan Stadium and were making their way up Nohingu Stratis. It suddenly occured to Mikita that the Peers were inside the old Zip building, directly on her left.

"Kané, the Peers, my friends, they were on the TV just now?"

"Yeah... and?"

"Well, they'll be right there. In the old Zip studios." She pointed to the station building.

And just as she raised her index finger, through the front door of the Zip building burst the Peers. They were all there: Marcie, Cy, Toora, Linden, Newton and Ellery. And being followed by Reg Spalding.

"Marcie! Toora! Over here!" shouted Mikita.

The Peers saw Mikita and ran over to her.

"Mikita, thank Herra it's you," said Marcie. "Look. There's no time to explain, but we've got rid of our GC abilities. The guy behind us is Reg Spalding. Deck him, if you would."

"Gotcha," replied Mikita.

She summoned up the GC and dealt Spalding a blow that sent his legs out from under him.

Spalding let loose and oath too ribald for print and crumpled to the ground like a rag doll.

Kané sent a shot of blazing yellow towards the shyster that caught him full on the jaw and sent him shooting up and onto the roof of the TV station. He landed safely, hanging like an Earth-based scarecrow on the large Nu-Zip aerial.

"Oops," said Kané. "A bit strong, I think."

Marcie hugged Mikita for all she was worth. "We're so pleased to see you, Mikita. But your planet seems to be a bit of a shizzer at the moment. Thanks to your old President."

"Yeah. He's turned into some wild maniac. He's got Polo."

"Yes, we know. And now they're heading to Paradi

Square. Is that nearby?"

"Yes, it's just around the corner."

Marcie smiled. "Well, what are we waiting for?"

# Chapter 34
*16:53 - 13 October, 2187 (Muhaze, Tapi-36)*

"So, Jon-7. Tell us. How are you going to get us the moon you said we could have?"

Jon-7 shook his head. "Look, Grissh. I've been in jail. I lost the election, old chum. I can't get you the moon, you know that."

"The Froome always stick to their word. A deal is a deal. You promised us Kloq-888, you need to get us it."

"But mate, I can't. I've told you a hundred times. Look at me. I'm a prisoner. Well, was a prisoner…"

"Yeah, and you haven't thanked us for that, either!"

"No, well… I mean. Yeah, thanks Grissh." He turned to the rest of The Froome. "Thanks, everyone."

The Froome mumbled some stuff like: 'too late now' and 'about draining time', and so on.

"Where are we going, Grissh?" shouted Bardroola, from the front of the truck. Then added: "Herra, there's mutants everywhere!"

Grisshum looked around the street. Bardroola was right. He'd never seen so many mutants all in the same place. And they all looked very perturbed.

"Hmmm… Oh well, let's follow the mutant-dudes and see what's shaking! Anyone ready for an adventure?"

The Froome responded in the affirmative and

159

Bardroola revved the engine of the flat-bed.

Grisshum gave Bardroola the thumbs up. "Sounds good, 'Droola! Let's go!"

## Chapter 35
*16:59 - 13 October, 2187 (Starship Argon, Lumiol-S3 Apex, Michael 6 Quadrant)*


Tina Gössner pressed the door of Holly's room and entered carefully. The unconscious guard outside the cell was testament to Tina's suspicion of Reg Spalding and his motives.

Holly was still unconscious, but was talking to herself.

"Engage... Crossing Point... Can't get there..."

Tina stroked her forehead and Holly soon stopped her chatter. She felt around her body but found nothing. She checked her scalp, nothing there too. But around the back of her neck, Tina found the lump that told her the whole story. She buzzed Jameson.

"Captain, Holly Dreamo's been bugged. Spalding's been up to his tricks."

"Good work, Tina. Get her down to Medical. I'll meet you there."

"Roger, Phil."

## Chapter 36
*17:05 - 13 October, 2187 (Starship Krashaon, Michael 6 Quadrant)*

Zanthu was packing for the seminary. He'd already put on the habit supplied to him by the priests - a brown affair with a leather belt inscribed with his Scyfer. It would be a long year with the holy men. They were stern, not without humour but pious, as one would expect.

Zanthu realised he'd made mistakes. The mistakes of youth, and a hot-headed youth, at that. Thinking that he could bring Mikita into his own world and have her accepted immediately, had been callow. And now he'd lost Mikita, and lost the respect he once had in his community. He would have a hard job of convincing his people that he was fit for any sort of government position on his return. As the son of Qaanhu X he was expected to carry on the ways of the Codes, not tamper with them. He'd been a fool. And now he was paying the price.

There was a knock at the door.

"Come in," said Zanthu, morosely.

The door slid open and there was his brother, Leylaan.

Zanthu smiled. "Leylaan, a friendly face at last."

"Yes, but that is all I can give you. You're leaving in half an hour. I was told to come and tell you."

Zanthu nodded. "Thanks, brother, I'm almost ready."

"Yes, I can see you are dressed for the journey."

Zanthu nodded. "I am, indeed."

"Zanthu, can we talk?"

"Of course, what do you wish to talk about?"

"Mikita."

Zanthu's smile disappeared. "There's nothing to talk about concerning her."

"On the contrary, Zanthu, I feel there is."

"If you're going to tell me to follow my heart, and all that rubbish, then you can leave right now."

"Ah, there you go again, dear brother."

"What do you mean?"

"Your stubbornness. Just like father. It's a curse. Can't take the advice of the people close to you. And never mind a bit of mild criticism."

"No. You're wrong, Leylaan. I can take criticism."

"I'm sorry, little brother. You cannot. And this is what holds you back from achieving your desires. Ever since we were children it has been this way. And now that both mother and father are gone... well, let's just say we both need to change and step up to the duties that are asked of us. I have received word from Marcie, my friend, the Peer, that they have found a way of reversing the Golden Circuit - a way to rid oneself of its power. I propose to follow this procedure, and become a normal being again. She tells me they are encouraging all GC wielders to do the same."

"That sounds wonderful, Leylaan. I am pleased for you. I can see in your eyes that this has made you truly happy."

"It has, dear brother. It has."

"And I suppose you will take over father's role afterwards?"

"Yes. I will. But it will take time for me to convince the Elders that I am now without the GC power. That will be some task. But I will succeed."

"Yes, I know you will."

"Zanthu, do not give up. On Mikita, I mean. I know she still loves you. In a way, I know her better than you. Funny, isn't it? The time we spent together on Plaateux-5, we learnt so much there. Not all of it bad, despite what the Guardians had in mind."

Zanthuu paused, deep in thought. "You may be right,

Leylaan. But I cannot let myself think there is hope for Mikita and me. It is too early for that. I have a year to sit out in the seminary. I can't let my thoughts become clouded with false hopes."

"A year is a long time. But perhaps I can get this shortened, after I become Leader."

Zanthu looked up at his brother. "You would do that?"

"Of course. I would then fight for you to become my Second. You are my brother. I will need your advice."

Zanthu smiled.

"But look, it is time. We must go. Come, let's proceed to the Holdings."

Zanthu fastened the top of his pack and slung it over his shoulder. It was very lightweight, he was not allowed to take much with him.

"Oh, but before you go, I have a surprise for you."

Leylaan, pressed the door switch, and there outside was Spoolu, his Muidog. Spoolu's tail was wagging like a flag in a gale.

"I thought you might like to see her before you left," said Leylaan.

Zanthu rushed forward, dropping his pack as he did so. He bent done to hug his dog.

"Thank you, Leylaan. You are a true friend."

Leylaan smiled. "I think she misses Marta. What do you think?"

"Well, we shall see if we can't reunite you both... at some point... in the future, maybe."

"Come, brother. We must go."

Zanthu grabbed the muidog under her ears. "I'll be back Spoolu. Make sure you look after Leylaan for me."

The muidog, barked a reply, as her tail continued to wag.

# Chapter 37
*17:13 - 13 October, 2187 (Starship Argon, Lumiol-S3 Apex, Michael 6 Quadrant)*

"It's a Nano-Grem," said Gadget. "Used to make your subject obey your every command and listen in to your surroundings, conversations and so on. Old tech. I'm surprised Spalding would be using it. And it looks like it's burnt out."

"Perhaps the fire has got too close to the source."

"How so, Dr. Gössner?" asked Jameson.

"The GC, Holly's been trying to access it. I heard her mumbling in her sleep. Maybe it has something to do with the burn out."

"Could be, Doctor," replied Gadget. "The power generated by the GC is formidable. Enough to light up a small city."

Jameson paused. "What did you just say?"

"The power generated by the GC -"

"No, after that."

"Enough to light up a small city... Why, Captain. What is it?"

"I've just worked out what Spalding is up to. Gadget get on to Ω. Plot course for Tapi-36. Full power!"

## Chapter 38
*17:33 - 13 October, 2187 (Muhaze, Tapi-36)*

All eyes were on Sempre at the top of the monument in Paradi Square.

Sempre had Polo by the throat. She was gasping for air.

Hundreds of mutants were gathered at the base of the huge statue, their eyes swirling around inside there heads. They were chanting: 'Sempre, Sempre, Sempre' very quietly, but the sound of all the voices together was loud, and the repetition maddening.

Mikita and Kané pushed their way through the mob, hoping against hope to reach the front of the crowd and do something, *anything*, to help their cousin.

The Froome and Jon-7 and Budgie stood on the open-back truck watching.

Overhead, the Turandot hovered, while inside Jameson and his crew looked on at the scene.

From his aerial aerial view, Reg Spalding could see the former TAPCON boss, like some Earth-based King Kong - hunted by everyone - and he laughed. He laughed at the situation, but even more he laughed at himself. For being such a fool.

The Police had already arrived at the scene and had

begun to set up snipers with drug-guns. But it was difficult to get a clear shot at Sempre because he was flailing around all over the place, and also because he held Polo in front of himself.

Sempre was screaming: "I want Swish and Tamashito here, now! Or the girl gets it!"


Back at the TV studio, Phinn and Harriet were finding it difficult controlling themselves.

"I can't believe what I'm seeing, Harriet!" said Phinn.

"Yes, I know, Phinn. I can't believe it either!" she said, glibly. For once, Harriet's cynical mask had dropped.


Mikita and Kané were slowly moving through the crowd of mutants. Mikita didn't know what she would do when they got to the front, she only hoped that she could get close enough to do *something* before it was too late.

Then, on top of the monument, Sempre picked up Polo and held her aloft, high above his head. He lunged forward towards the edge of the railings and began to scream again: "Go away! Or I'll drop the girl!"

Milksilk was on the radio to his snipers. "Does anyone have a shot at him?"

One voice came back. It was Pritchard. "I've got him, Captain."

"Good, shoot when ready."

Milksilk's second in command was standing beside him: "But Captain, the girl. He's going to drop the girl."

"I don't care about the girl!" he replied. "We need to take down Sempre!"

A shot rang out from the rooftops. A dart hit Sempre in the shoulder. He winced in pain, but still he stood firm.

"Again!" shouted Milksilk. "Fire again! Any of you, shoot the draining thing!"

Several more shots rang out and Sempre began to stumble with their impact.

"Again! Hit it again!" shouted Milksilk, hysterically, as more darts flew across the sky.

Sempre moved backwards and forwards, teetering woozily as the darts' poison began to take hold of his nervous system. He tripped up over his own feet (or rather, his mother's) and lurched toward the protective barrier. His arms crashed down on the railings and he lost control of Polo. Her body rolled over, along Sempre's arms, and she was sent over the edge.

She let out a piercing scream as she hurtled towards the pavement below.

## Chapter 39
*Earlier that day - 13 October, 2187 (Muhaze, Tapi-36)*


But wait.
Let us stop here for a moment.


It might be too obvious to say that the past chain of events have had a distinct aroma of coincidence about them - what with our characters criss-crossing back and forth across the coordinates of time and space, turning up unexpected, at unusual moments. There certainly would seem to be a strong element of chance attached to the proceedings. So to make up for all that, things are about to get quite spectacularly providential...


Earlier that day, when Kané had sold Polo's watch and black box to Keith, the pawn shop owner, little did he realise the repercussions of his actions. For in that moment in time he set off a series of events that, unfortunately for him, would lead to his now very imminent death.

Keith had closed 'Keith's Used and Collectables' early, then got on the phone to several of his contacts in the collecting business. Keith knew he had a wallet-busting opportunity and he was keen to get the maximum

169

price for his efforts. He was about to start a bidding war between three of the major players in antiquities in the entire Quadrant: Genevieve Gluut, an alien from Fuschia-2609(b), Exwye Z, a trader from Yolanda-CDI and Wolton Wong, an ex-Earthling with many high-up connections across Michael-6, and by far the big favourite for the sale. Keith phoned round his trio of wanna-haves and gave them an hour to sort out their bids. He then called them back on his conference line, opened a fresh bag of Flooreati's chips, and began the auction:

"OK, everyone. Can you hear me alright? Genevieve?"

"Yah, Keef. You bet your buns."

"Exwye?"

"Yuss, Keev. I is here."

"And Wolton, you there?"

"Oh, yeah, baby! I'm here, Keith! Gonna win this guys, so get outta my way!"

"OK, flick to screen-view, bidders."

Keith's screen came alive with the images of the three bidders.

Exwye looked very rough, like he'd had a hard night on the Cosmic Stock Market. His spiked-up hair was matted and his face lined. But he'd put on a tie and polished the Aug that was inserted into his eye socket - an old injury from an ambush of Grintxs when he was a runner.

Wolton had clearly put on a lot of weight recently, his black hair was buzzed short, making his podgy face even more so, while a grey t-shirt, that read 'Keep Calm And Use Napalm', was barely covering his bulging stomach.

Genevieve looked the same as she always did - shoulder-length green hair with a straight fringe, three eyes, blue skin, petite frame. She spoke first: "Oooh, Wolton, honey, you been on the pies, yah?" she said.

Wolton was incredulous. "Hey, Genny! Look at Keith, before you get too carried away. He's got so fat that if he cut himself, gravy would come out!"

Keith blushed a bit and hid his Doreati's behind his back.

"Wolton! I thought you were my friend?"

Wong shook his head. "Friend? I have no friends. At

least, not in the buying and selling business."

Keith was hurt. "I don't know if I want to sell you these things now, after all that."

"Oh come on, girls," said Exwye. "I need to get this Aug fixed at 2pm, it's giving me awful wind. Can we get on with this, please?"

"Well, if Genevieve and Wolton would control themselves, we could," said Keith.

"Well, I'm ready. Let's go," said Genevieve.

"Times a-wasting," replied Wolton.

"Right then," said Keith. He then placed Kané's items in full view of the screen.

"I have before me the two objects I told you about. One is a black onyx box. Highly polished, perfect condition and very, very rare. Though I don't need to tell you that.'

"Looks good, Keith," said Wolton. "Who'd you get it from?"

Keith grinned. "Ah, I'm sorry, Wolton. You know I can't reveal my sources."

"No, you never do," said Exwye. "So tiresome…"

"Well, if I did, Exwye, how on Tapi-36 could I sell you these things at such inflated prices?"

"That's for sure," replied Genevieve.

"Yes, well, item two is even more exciting. An Earth-based Mouse watch." Keith brought the watch right up to the scanner on his desktop. "LOOK. AT. THIS." It brought some 'ooohs' and 'aaahs' from the triumvirat of dealers.

"Not too shabby, Keith," said Wolton.

"Very nice," said Genevieve.

"Meh," said Exwye, clearly hiding his real enthusiasm behind a pretend nonplussed mien.

"Good. I'm glad you're all interested. Let's start with the box. Can I begin the bidding at $500."

"Muhazian?" asked Wolton.

"Oh, yes, pardon me. $500 Muhazian, ladies and gentlemen."

"She ain't no lady," said Wolton.

"And you ain't no gentleman, Wolton."

"Works for me," he replied, with a smile.

Keith butted in. "Do I hear $600?"

171

"$600," said Exwye.

"Thank you. Do I hear $700?"

"$700," replied Genevieve.

"Thank you, Genny. Do I hear $800?

"$2,000!" It was Wolton Wong.

"Um, sorry Wolton, did you say $2,000?"

"Yep, take it or leave it."

"Well, Exwye? Genevieve? Either of you interested in $2,100?"

"Nope," said Exwye. "Not worth that much."

"Uh-uh. Wolton can have it, at that price," said Genevieve. "Way over the mark. But hang on, what do you know that we don't, Wolton? It's unlike you to bid so far over retail."

"No. Nothing you don't know. Just a feeling I have for black onyx. In the future, I mean. Five, ten years time, this baby is gonna break the bank."

"Not a chance," said Exwye.

"I think he's lost it," said Genevieve.

"Well, wait and see, folks. Wait and see."

"We shall," said Exwye, haughtily.

Keith was keen to get a move on. "In that case, sold at $2,000 to Wolton Wong."

Wolton looked pleased. The others didn't know of his plans to buy up all the black onyx, with the help of several big dealers across the Quadrant.

"Now, on to the Earth-based watch. A fine, fine piece this one. Immaculate condition, and still in its box.

"Ever been taken *out* of the box?" asked Exwye.

"Not to my knowledge," replied Keith, forgetting to say that his knowledge concerning the provenance of the watch was profoundly limited. "The seal is still intact." He held the box up again to show them.

"Thank you," said Exwye. "Now we will see who will have the best toy."

"Not going to be you, Exwye," said Wolton.

Keith began the bidding. "OK, do I hear $5,000 Muhazian for this beauty?"

"$5,000," said Genevieve.

"5.1," said Exwye.

"Oh, come, come children," said Wolton. "Surely we go up in $1,000s?

172

There was a pause from the other two until Exwye and Genevieve agreed.

"$6,000," said Exwye.

"7," from Wolton.

"8," from Genevieve.

"Exwye?"

"That's me out, Keith," said Exwye, "See ya around, guys."

And with that he turned off his screen. Now there were only faces of Genevieve and Wolton left on Keith's monitor"

"Wolton, do I hear $9,000?"

"Of course," said Wolton. "$9,000 smackeroonies. Genevieve?"

"You're busting my maracas, Wolton. But... OK, $10,000."

Keith was metaphorically rubbing his hands in glee. This was way more than he had imagined he would get for the watch. Way, way more.

Wolton did not hesitate. "11."

But Genevieve was done. "Sorry, boys. 10 was my best offer. Gotta go." Genevieve flicked her screen off to leave Wolton's chubby visage beaming at Keith.

"Well done, Walton. That's a cool $13,000 for the two. You want me to ship them out to you, or you want to send someone round to pick 'em up?"

"Yeah, Keith. I got a man in Muhaze. In fact, he's on his way to you now."

"That confident were you?"

"Oh, yes. Genevieve and Exwye are no competition. Not with my backers. Anyway, thanks Keith. As always, a pleasure."

Wolton turned off at his end. The screen went blank at Keith's.


Wolton's courier arrived about ten minutes later, just as Keith had finished the packing up of the items. The man transferred the funds over to Keith and left the shop.


Five minutes later, the same man turned the corner at

Paradi Square and saw a crowd of people gathering underneath the Atlas Statue. He looked to see what was happening, but as he took his eyes off the road a pedestrian, who was rushing to catch a glimpse of the spectacle, ran in front of his vehicle. The man slammed on the brakes but managed to clip the pedestrian (who was a teenager of quite sizeable build) on the hip. This started the youth spinning around and clutching at his leg in some considerable pain. He then proceeded to fall towards the ground, but not before knocking someone else over, who in turn knocked someone else, and so on, like a set of dominoes. This set up a wave of tumbling bodies through the crowd.

The timing was perfect. For at that very moment Sempre lost all sense of reality from the darts venom, and dropped Polo from the top of the tower.

Kané, standing at the front of the crowd was directly in line of the all-consuming wave of falling people, and was pushed forwards and down, towards the concrete in front of him. His body erupted in a shriek of golden power that shot out from the top of his skull.

"Kané!!" screamed Mikita. "Oh, Kané..."

However, Polo was lucky. She caught the force full on her midriff and was sent spiralling through the air, landing in the canvas awning of a new Gretchi's that had just opened up that morning. A fractured collarbone and some whiplash were the only injuries she sustained.

A chopper had managed to lasso the, by now, heavily sedated Sempre and he was soon brought down to the ground and taken away to a secure-zone in the Muhaze Hospital. Tamashito was called in, and Sempre's body and head of Mayette Froome were brought in from the airfield. Very carefully, may I add.

But then...

**Chapter 40**
17:45 - 13 October, 2187 (Muhaze, Tapi-36)

"Stop!" shouted a voice. "Stop what you're doing!"
It seemed like the voice was coming from...
*everywhere.*
The crowd fell silent.
The mutants froze.
In fact, *everyone* froze. Everyone, that is, except for
our favourite characters: Mikita, Polo up in the awning,
Gompi, Charly, The Froome. Jon-7 and Budgie were all
*compos mentis.*
They all looked around.
Time was standing still.
Then, a face appeared on the megatron.
"Peter?" said Mikita, in surprise.
His image then disappeared from the megatron and
suddenly Peter was standing in the Square before the
crowd.
"Hello, my friends," he began, then noticed their
astonished looks. "Oh, don't look so surprised. Who did
you expect it to be? Aldoorin, Gildan, some other bore.
Or Florina, she was nice. Hanoi Jones, perhaps? The
muidogs? Yes, the animals in charge of the humans!
Brilliant! But, no. It's just me. So, give me your full
attention. The Lines Of Incidence are already drawn up -

175

well, being drawn up - but suffice to say, I am here as the hand that makes the water ripple on the surface of a lake; the overseer of the cosmos, the Golden Circuit, whatever you want to call it. I am like a mirror of millions of Peters, all different, all the same, spiraling down into a place where wisdom and thought do not function. There, only the metaphysical exists. Even I cannot remember or understand my origin, whether I am really a man or a woman, a beast or an angel. Only that I am in charge of this level of consciousness. There are others, in other places, of course." Peter paused, and put on a wistful gaze. "I had hopes for the Guardians. I must say, their ways were impressive. But they blew it. So now I must hand over my control to one of you. You see, friends, my time here is up. My work here is done. And not very well, may I add. And all I can say about that is: 'Oops.' But whosoever takes on my job will have to make a better fist of it than I did. That is a given. Otherwise who knows where we might end up? Who knows what might befall the human and aliens races. So, there we go. Now, who wants it? Who wants to run the cosmos? Anyone? Jon-7?"

The former Froome boss couldn't resist the temptation of omnipotence. "Yes, I'll have it!" he replied, a bit too quickly.

Peter shook his head. "No. Wrong answer, I'm afraid. Not you."

Jon-7 began to sulk.

"Anyone else? Mikita, do you want it?"

Mikita shook her head. "Not a chance, Peter. Not in a million years."

"Correct. How about you, Polo?"

Polo raised her head above the awning. "Absolutely not!"

"Correct, again. So it's not either one of the Smith girls!" Peter paused for a second or two, then started in at them again. "C'mon, you all look like you've been playing a game and suddenly someone's changed the rules. Well? *Somebody* have a guess as to who it might be!"

"Is it Captain Jameson?" asked Mikita.

"No. Next!"

"Is it Dr. Gössner?" asked Polo.

"No."

"Is it me?" asked Budgie.

"That's a joke, right?"

"Is it Charly?" asked Polo.

"Oooooh, you're getting warm!"

"Is it Gompi?" asked Bardroola.

"Yes! We have a winner! It *is* Gompi! Well done Bardroola!"

They all turned to look at the embarrassed mutant.

Gompi looked around at everyone, mouth agape.

"Well, Gompi?" asked Mikita. "Will you accept Peter's offer?"

Gompi grinned. "Yes, I take."

"Correct!" shouted Peter. "That is the correct answer!"

"Wait a second," said Jon-7. "You're giving the reigns of the universe to a mutant?"

"Ah, but Mr. Potts, you see, he is not just *any* mutant. Gompi is an error. A spectacularly wonderful error! The Specialists really goofed up when they made him - and they goofed up when making Charly, too. And now the two of them will be given my powers and my duties. Flitting here and there, doing good, righting wrongs, having a laugh, and generally making sure that the good guys beat the bad guys – every time, not just once in awhile like I've been able to do. Hmmmm... You know, the more I think about it, the worse I seem to have done in my tenure. But let's not dwell on the past, shall we? Now then, let's not hang around any longer than we need to. Gompi. Charly. Please step forward."

The two mutants did as Peter asked. Then stood nervously as he raised his arms above his head.

The Golden Circuit grew up from his inner core, out to his fingertips, then enveloped the two mutants, but suddenly Gompi waved him off.

"Wait! Peter, you stop!"

Peter lowered his hands. "What? What is it, Gompi? What is wrong?" he asked.

"We put in application for little Gompi. Yesterday at Clinic."

"Yes," replied Peter. "And?"

"Can we keep little one? Can we do this 'saving

universe' and keep little baby mutant?"

Peter smiled. "Yes, of course you can. But it is hard work being a parent *and* having complete control of the cosmos. You will need to love each other very much to succeed."

Gompi looked at Charly. "Oh, that no problem, Mr. Peter."

Charly blushed.

"Good, Now, where was I?"

"You were doing the GC thing, Peter," said Polo.

"Yes, so I was. Thank you, Miss Smith."

Peter raised his hands again and brought forth the Golden Circuit. He then made a little 'abracadabra' kind of speech, and at the end of it, everyone cheered - and then... they all went home.

## Epilogue

And so, David Sempre's head was finally reunited with his body, and Mayette Froome's body was finally reunited with her head.

Dr. Tam had done an excellent job.

A few days later, in a touching moment of reunification, Mayette Froome turned to her son and, to Sempre's great surprise, hugged him.

Sempre didn't know what to do.

It was the first time in his life that he could remember ever being held by his mother.

"I'm so sorry, David," she said, her voice trembling a little in it's new larynx. "I'm so sorry that your father and I were not very good parents. We did what we thought was right. Unfortunately, it was deemed a violation of Cosmic Human Rights and an international crime to the Universe, but... ah well, it's tough at the top." She hugged him again, then looked at him, lovingly, and kissed him on the brow.

A tear of joy ran down Sempre's cheek. That's all he'd ever wanted - someone to love him. And preferably his own mum or dad.

Janeee Swish came forward and put the handcuffs onto Sempre's now more manly wrists, as two policeman moved in to lead Mayette Froome and her son away to jail.

The Peers went home. Back to their respective planets, now free to be the regular children they'd always wanted to be. No longer burdened by the Golden Circuit. Not special. Not gifted. Well, only in as much as they were human, and the possessors of minds and hearts capable of extraordinary compassion and understanding.

*

Meanwhile, Mikita mourned her brother, and Polo mourned her cousin.

There would be no bringing Kané back with the GC.

Mikita also mourned the loss of another person, in a different way, of course.

Zanthu.

Perhaps one day they would see each again. But that was for the future to decide...

*

The Froome and Jon-7 went their separate ways. Jon-7 ended up working at "Dishes With Fishes', Budgie's old job. It was all he could get - given his skill set.

And Budgie now co-hosted 'Late Lunch with Kendall' or rather 'Kendall & Budgie In the Afternoon', as it was now called.

The Froome opened a restaurant.

*

Jameson and the crew? Well, they went back to work.

The ISF was renamed The Cosmic Peace Alliance, and things were progressing slowly...

*

But more importantly...

The evening after the Sempre siege, Gompi and Charly went to the Repro-Life Clinic and picked up their new baby mutant. In fact, to their surprise and extreme delight,

180

the Repro people had done an extra one for them.

A baby girl.

They had originally wanted to call the boy Chico, but then they remembered that boy mutants need to have an 'i' on the end of their names. So, instead, they named him Harvi, after Gompi's grandfather-mutant. The mutant-server typed the name into the 'Database of Mutants' and he was officially born. They named the girl 'Charly 2'.

Outside the clinic, Peter was waiting for them. He looked very frail and tired.

"Come my children," he began, his voice creaking like a rusty gate. "I don't have much time left... And you have much to learn." He looked up at little Harvi and Charly 2, and smiled a very crinkly smile, then said: "They are perfect. You are *all* so perfect."

A qi-bird flew down from a nearby tree and landed on Gompi's shoulder. It began to sing a song of such delight that time seemed to stand still. And as the moon began to rise, so it hummed a low, rolling bassline, while the stars twinkled out a glockenspiel-like *cantus firmus*, and very soon, the rest of the heavenly orchestra had joined in, each astral instrument proclaiming the mutants everlasting love.

Gompi smiled at Charly, and they both looked down adoringly at their two children. The universe was now moving in sympathy with their thoughts - when they smiled, the fading sun shone; when they laughed, the heavens danced with joy.

The qi-bird's song continued, and everything swirled into the landscape in a spiral of colour and sound that transported them skywards, on to a place where only the God's played, myths were created, and where they had no commercials on TV - and all was well in the Michael-6 Quadrant.

Then, somewhere far away, a man in a dark suit and dark glasses smiled...


THE END

181

## About The Author

John K. Irvine currently lives in Edinburgh, Scotland with a beautiful wife and two children, none of whom can abide modern jazz... but he still lets them live with him.

His poetry and short stories have been published, or are forthcoming, in: Poetry Scotland, Open Mouse, Blinking Cursor, Essence, Ink, Sweat & Tears, A Handful of Stones, South and Streetcake Magazine, amongst others.

'Sempre's Return' is the third and final novel in 'The Smith Chronicles' series.

For more information please go to:

www.johnirvinewordsandmusic.com